LINEAGE

By M.K. Parsons

*For the persuaders and the influencers
and the roots of mighty trees.*

Prologue

I was thirty seconds late. I – Morris Koenig, born for the specific purpose of saving the past – was thirty seconds too late to save the most important person in the world.

It wouldn't have been as bad if I'd been a full hour or a day late, would it? But I was only seconds off in my calculations, and because of it, Jamie was taken.

My grandmother, Arabella Eisen, would remind me I shouldn't have been there in the first place. *Morris, it was an Unalterable, and you wouldn't have loved that girl as much if she didn't have to walk that path.*

I wasn't convinced that fate had prevented Jamie's rescue.

I ran from the top of the hill through the wilderness of Central Park. Overhead, the night sky flashed with the angry colors of a passing comet. I slipped over the black rock formations and gouged my arms and legs, but I didn't stop. In front of me, I saw Joe grab the skinny arm of a defiant little girl. He shoved her into a long line of kids dressed in early American clothing. As they stood in front of the timeship, they screamed in terror. Maybe they thought Joe had come from the comet. But whatever they didn't understand, I could tell they knew Joe was bad news.

"Jamie!" I cried her name, but the timeship's engine roared to life, overpowering every other sound. I fell to my knees, my lungs screaming for air, my wounds on fire. But the cuts and bruises couldn't compare to my frustration. I roared in anger as the timeship disappeared in the vintage New York sky.

"I'm sorry, Jamie," I whispered. "I wanted to save you."

One

Transient Village, Manhattan
September, 2094

My friends and I wouldn't have admitted it, but we loved the nights when the SkyJack ships appeared. The war was a welcome distraction from our boring existence. Battle was freeing. Victory was the ultimate rush.

We paraded through the woods, obnoxiously loud. We'd wake the entire village, but so what? We'd won. The SkyJacks looked tough, but they never had a plan. The Transient, on the other hand, had a plan for everything.

I admit I didn't mind the kills. I'd read enough history to know that New Yorkers hadn't always been so savage, but I didn't mind ending worthless SkyJacks. They weren't the same as us, and all they wanted to do was destroy us. I just imagined them hurting my grandmother. Then it was easy to pull the trigger.

But a secret corner of my psyche wanted to be better than this. We'd probably be better human beings if we didn't have to constantly kill to survive.

I was eighteen, and I'd spent my entire life in the Transient village. My grandmother, Arabella Eisen, had raised me. At the same time, our people had built the Transient village and our way of life.

I'd be leader one day. Grandma liked reminding me. It was my duty to be as mindful as the Transient adults. My responsibility was not only for our future, but our past. It was a burden I didn't like to think about.

Killing SkyJacks was easier.

"Morris Koenig, and you going to dance with me?" A playful female voice called from the other side of the bonfire we'd built. A boy had brought out his bongo drum and another had a guitar, and the song they played matched our spirits. I threw a few more logs on the fire and went to join the girl. I took her hands and began to dance as the Transient youth dance, a complex flurry of motion as controlled as everything else in our way of life.

After the dance ended, I slipped my arms around her waist and held her, enjoying the way she felt. Any other eighteen-year-old boy liked it as much, but my gift made girls more of a temptation to me. I could easily misuse my power of influence. I could convince nearly anyone to do what I wanted. It gave me a heady feeling in moments like these, when I was still on fire from the battle and already experiencing the rush of victory.

As much as I loved the feeling of power, there were consequences to my ability. Because it was so easy for me to make people do things, sometimes without intending to, I could never be sure someone's favor was genuine. This bothered me more and more as I got older, though I never discussed it with anyone else. I didn't want to manipulate love. My desire was to be liked for me, and be liked all the time – not just when my current crush was close enough in proximity to be under my spell.

I stared out into the brush at the edge of the Transient village. As I turned in the ashes by the fire, holding the Transient girl tighter than I should, I saw the flash of someone's eyes.

My eyes tried to adjust to the dim light of the forest. I was able to make out her face. She was watching us, crouched where she probably figured we'd never see her. But how could I miss that mind of hers? She didn't have a chance against the empathic abilities I inherited from my mom.

She had exaggerated the effect of her flashing eyes with a line of kohl that extended nearly to her hairline. Her mouth was painted blood red, and the wildness of her ash-blonde hair stood apart from her head like a halo.

How ironic, since it was clear she was a SkyJack.

I stopped dancing and watched her. But she bolted the moment I took a step. I thought I had scared her, but when I turned around, I realized the others were watching her, too.

"Who does she think she is?" The girl I'd been holding scoffed in disbelief.

"Come on," another boy my age called. He held up his dirt-encrusted laser rifle. "Let's get her!"

My hesitation confused me. They turned to me, the unofficial leader. They'd been taught to defer to me since we were children. But they didn't wait for me to make up my mind. As the first boy took off into the woods, the rest followed him, taking up their weapons.

But my indecision held me in place. I shook my head, arguing with myself. I'd seen SkyJacks toy with victims before they killed them, as if it wasn't enough to defeat their prey, they must torture them first and cause as much suffering as they could.

It was their way. It was why we didn't hesitate to kill them first. Their general, Joe, taught them to live according to their desires. They could destroy anyone who got in their way, as long as they remained subject to his authority. In fact, it wasn't uncommon to come upon SkyJacks fighting each other for an animal kill or even the best place at the fire.

"Never – ever – ever – trust a sky dweller," my grandmother always said. "They know how to manipulate. They'll trick you. None of them care about your life or our people. Don't ever give them an inch of your trust."

Until this moment, I hadn't questioned it. I'd seen it for myself. But now, though not sure exactly why, I wanted to give this little SkyJack a chance.

In one exhilarating moment of decision, I took off in the opposite direction of the other fighters. I followed her tracks as far as the Collect Pond, where I saw the glint of metal snaps trailing her tight black pants. She had gone to the top of a thirty-foot Hangmen's Elm. Her boots swayed slightly in the air above me.

Fortunately, I was the quickest and quietest tree climber in the village. I figured it was Roxy's blood flowing through me. In minutes, I was behind her on the limb, close enough to grab her if needed. I made sure my footing was steady and my other arm was attached to the limb above before I spoke.

"I saw you watching us."

She whirled around, nearly losing her balance. But she caught herself and stood, grasping a sturdy branch above her with one hand. With the other, she pointed an impressive bronzed laser rifle to my face.

I barely noticed the gun because of her eyes. They hid within the garish fringed hair that was braided in alternating layers down her back and interwoven with a red silk ribbon. Beneath the dark makeup I read her cautious curiosity. I liked that she was interested in me. I hoped it was genuine and not just my annoying gift.

"So are you going to give me a reason not to drag you back and let the council have you?"

I was hoping to intimidate her, but it didn't work. She scoffed. "Are you going to give me a reason to use this?" She waved the gun in my face, reminding me who had the upper hand.

"How about we both put down our guns and talk?" I smiled, laying on the charm as thick as I could. The Transient girls would have been putty in my hands with far less effort. But this stubborn little SkyJack curled her lip and climbed up further, her gun still trained at my head.

"I don't put down my gun for my own kind, let alone Transient filth." She glanced at the sky. "Why don't you get down from the tree like a good little village boy and go away. I'll try hard not to shoot you in the back."

"Fine," I said. "But I'm not leaving until you tell me why you were watching us."

I saw a flicker of something in her expression. Was it vulnerability? It made her seem young. She had to be younger than me – maybe sixteen or seventeen? Young enough she shouldn't be so hardened.

As if she could read my thoughts, she scowled at me. "What do you think I was doing? Scouting for Joe. Thinking up ways to destroy you and your village."

I shook my head. "Not true."

"How do you know?"

I shrugged and tapped my forehead. "I can read minds. I know it's not true."

She had no response. I assumed she'd heard of Transient telepathy. She flitted past me and swung down from the branches like the Tibetan monkeys that roamed the Manhattan forest, descendants of Central Park Zoo monkeys set free when Joe leveled the city.

The girl didn't turn around again. I watched until she disappeared from the path and listened until I couldn't hear her chains clanging as she sprinted.

"What are you doing up there?" I heard my friend, Eric, call to me. They'd found me. As they ran after the girl, I yelled, hoping they would stop.

But inevitably, they caught up with her. I heard laser fire and saw her go down. She made a valiant attempt to get up and run on her obviously injured leg, but they overtook her, laughing as they threw her on the ground and tied her up like an animal. She screamed in pain and shouted curses at them.

"Look at the stitching on her coat. She's important to Joe." Eric said.

"We might get a medal for turning her in," added the girl I had danced with earlier.

They surrounded her and walked back to the village, talking about the great catch. The girl limped in fuming agony as they urged her on. When they passed me, I got a few reproachful glares. I knew I'd be getting a lecture from my grandma later that night.

I went to the Arena lab, hoping to avoid my grandmother. I stayed late, calculating specs for a time travel project for class. It would be my final exam before I graduated from the Arena school. I was so involved in a particularly troublesome equation I didn't look up when Arabella come in.

"Grandma, I think I may have just solved it." I said as she came to me. "This could change everything about our time travel procedures."

She smiled, but I could tell she wasn't surprised. "Good. I didn't doubt you would."

Arabella Eisen didn't raise her voice or lose control of her emotions. My gift of influence over other people's emotions was useless with her because she always kept herself under perfect control. But when she was worried about me, she could make me feel regret. I hadn't ruled it out as her gift – imposing shame on others. She could make me feel like I was going to throw up over stupid things I did. I cringed for the avalanche of remorse about to come down on me.

"Your team brought in a girl after the battle." She leaned against the counter, perusing my strings of digital equations hovering in the air around us in 9-D motion.

"I know." I played it cool. Maybe she'd let it go if I didn't take her bait.

"I heard an interesting story. Did you separate from the group and attempt to help the girl escape back to the sky dwellers with information about our village?"

I didn't answer. I looked back over the equations and reminded myself how smart I was. Maybe, just maybe, my grandmother was wrong about the girl.

"Morris, I'm fair. I always give you the benefit of the doubt. So tell me why your friends thought you were trying to help our enemy destroy us."

I frowned. "I just wasn't convinced that girl was really the enemy."

She sighed, concern evident in her expression, and nodded slowly. "I just took a look at her. There's no doubt she's a sky dweller. She's spent the last two hours cursing every Transient member that comes within twenty feet of her, telling them exactly how she's going to kill them when she escapes. Tell me how she isn't your enemy."

"I can't really explain it." I shrugged and avoided her gaze. "I just felt connected to her. I've never felt anything like it."

She didn't speak for a long moment as she watched me. "Did you bond with her?"

I laughed in disbelief as I felt my cheeks warm. "Of course not."

She visibly relaxed. "Okay. So tell me why you feel that way."

She and I both knew I couldn't give her a reason beyond my feelings.

"Morris, you know how important you are. You will lead this village into the new age. They must be able to trust and respect you."

I nodded, fidgeting with the data center keyboard.

"I am not without sympathy for the sky dwellers. Most of them were stolen from time and brought here as young children. Joe has taught them to hate and manipulate. In a very real sense, it isn't their fault. But it doesn't make them safe. They've been conditioned to destroy us. We have to be vigilant. We can't let our emotions overtake good sense. That's especially true for leaders."

By every accounting of reason and logic, she was right. I gave her a short nod and didn't argue.

But something about the conversation rubbed me the wrong way.

Two

I didn't follow her home. I wanted to finish my project and avoid more awkward conversation.

Around two in the morning, I went to get something from the supply room below the Arena. I didn't think much of it. I'd been below the main floor alone in the dead of night before. I took an illumination rod with me, my brain occupied with new time travel theories.

I considered keeping the breakthrough to myself and coming up with another project for the final exam, but it was too late. I had to share it. For a fleeting moment, I considered all the things I could do and the places I could go if the tech remained my secret. As soon as the council got a hold of it, there'd be a million rules to get around. I felt a little miffed. I was the one who'd come up with it; I should get to use it however I wanted.

I sorted through a tub of meta-material cloaks to find the newer model I'd thrown in there a month before. I found it and held it up, running the special fabric through my fingers. I'd developed it myself. I wished I'd hidden it in my closet rather than donating it to the unappreciative collective.

I hoped the cloak would protect the interior of the time machine better than the old version. If the cylinder could be safer for the traveler, we could move through time and space with a more exact speed.

"There's only one reason anyone would need a meta cloak."

I whirled around, surprised by the voice. The SkyJack girl was glaring at me. She narrowed her eyes, which appeared much smaller and more human since her face had been washed. She wore a basic prison uniform. I almost gasped at how small and vulnerable she looked.

"You're working on a time machine, aren't you?" She eyed me suspiciously.

I nodded and stepped closer to the holding beam around her. "You're the girl from the woods. My name is Morris. Morris Koenig. What's yours?"

"I don't know." She shrugged.

"You don't know your name?"

"The general calls me Jamie. Jamie Salvatore."

I took another step toward her. "But that's not your name?"

"It was the name on the laser rifle he pulled out of stock and handed to me when he brought me here." She shrugged and smirked at me.

I recalled my grandmother's words. "Did he bring you here from another time?"

She gave a short nod and rolled her eyes as if I was stupid for having to ask.

"What year were you born?"

"I don't know. I was only six or seven, something like that. The general doesn't teach history class."

I came to the edge of the transparent light beam. "So tell me about your time. Maybe I can guess."

She sighed, apparently irritated by my persistence, but I thought I read a flicker of interest. "I had lots of brothers and sisters. Probably why I was so easy to take. My mother died in childbirth the year I was taken. We lived with my father in a house he built just inside the wall."

I perked up at the mention of a wall. "So there was a wall? Did you have electricity? Cars?"

She tilted her head as she considered the question. "No. Horses and carts. Mules. Lots of sheep."

"Was it this island? Manhattan?" I suspected so, because Joe wouldn't have been able to travel anywhere else in the Transient timeship he stole from our people. I doubted he would try to venture out from the island.

She nodded. "I remember the shape of the river."

"Anything else you remember?"

She tilted her head to the side and closed her eyes. "I remember something on the northern tip of the island. It was tall and wide and had large... propellers that turned in the wind."

"A windmill." I nodded confidently. "I know where you come from."

"How?" She stared at me skeptically.

"From my *History of Manhattan* course. You come from the earliest civilized time here – the seventeenth century. Most likely between 1650-1700."

"There was a comet," she said suddenly, as if it had just occurred to her. "The week before Joe showed up, there was a bright comet in the sky and every day it seemed to get bigger. Everyone was scared to death."

Morris went to the data center and entered the information. He looked back at her and smiled. "You were taken in 1680." I hesitated, wondering how she would respond to my idea. "I could stop him. Joe. If this tech works."

She was clearly interested for a second, but she shook her head. "Why does it matter?" she scoffed. "Your council will probably kill me, anyway."

I frowned. She hadn't come to Joe's army willingly. She'd been stolen and brainwashed so she'd be useful to him. She deserved a second chance.

Maybe they all did.

"I can talk them out of it." I held up the meta cloak. "So you know this tech?"

She shrugged. "Sure. I'm good with tech."

"What have you done?"

"Repaired the timeship a few times. And when no one's paying attention I work on my own projects." She nodded toward the cloak in my hand. "You must have found a way to make your time travel more exact. You could control the wormhole if you could go fast enough. But you'd have to survive the trip. Which explains the cloak."

I was stunned, but I tried not to show it. It had taken me five years of trial and error to come to understand my theory. She made it sound like old news.

"Does Joe have this tech?" I asked uncertainly.

She hesitated before she answered. Did I see a weakness under her tough exterior? "The general can't pull this off. Yet."

"But you can?" I was suspicious.

"I've always believed it was possible." She hesitated again, looking away. "But why give him the power to specifically choose where he steals kids? I kept it to myself."

I chewed on my lip, trying to decide what to do. Either she was trying to bait me into trusting her so she could use it against me, or she was telling the truth. Before I'd decided if it was a good idea, I had hit the release and the holding beam had shut down.

I pulled on her arm. "Come on. You can tell the council what you told me."

"It's not going to make a difference." She jerked her arm away. "Just because I don't trust the general doesn't make me your friend." She snarled at me as she took a step back. "If you let me go, I won't go back to the sky people. I'll find a survival village somewhere."

I remembered grandmother saying how manipulative SkyJacks could be. *They'll say anything, Morris. Don't believe a word. They're taught to lie and they're good at it.*

"Nope," I said, reaching for her arm again. "I don't trust the word of SkyJacks. If we let you live, it will be on our terms."

"I'll sneak away." She tried to shake off my grip, but I didn't let go.

I laughed. "You haven't met a Transient droid, I take it. Try to get past one of them and you'll regret it."

"Droid tech is the easiest to override. I've done it a thousand times." She raised an eyebrow.

Don't believe it. I took a step closer and let my face hover an inch away from hers. "I am going to try to save your life. In return, I expect you to be honest. Do you agree?"

I used my gift then, transferring a sense of calm I hoped would help her believe me. I watched in satisfaction as her expression softened and her mouth dropped open in surprise.

"What are you doing?" she asked in a breathless voice. I clearly heard the fear.

I had to fight temptation. This wasn't a good idea. I already felt different around her. If I lost control and used my gift to take something that didn't belong to me, it wouldn't end well.

You are not allowed to persuade anyone to do what benefits you. Your gift is not for your own advantage.

The memory of Grandmother's reminder was enough. I closed my eyes and steeled myself against the attraction I felt. I recognized that pull, not because I'd ever experienced it myself, but because I knew my parents had felt it. The attraction of opposites.

She staggered back as my mind released hers. "What was that? I feel sick."

She stared at me with accusation as I watched her. I'd never had a girl respond that way before – as if I was some sort of monster. I was curious about the difference, but I didn't comment on it.

"Do we have a deal?" I folded my arms across my chest.

She hesitated while I waited. Finally, her posture relaxed. "Fine."

"Good. Now help me solve this equation and I'll let you be the first test subject for the new cylinder."

She narrowed her eyes and I laughed. I beckoned her forward with a nod. "I'm just kidding. I call the first trip through." *And I'm going to 1680*, I added silently.

"Won't they be mad if I'm out of my prison?" Jamie glanced around.

I smiled and puffed up my chest a little. "I guess you don't know who I am."

"Are you in line for the Transient throne, then?" she quipped, a half-smile appearing on her face that made her seem almost childlike.

"Something like that." I walked back toward the door to the classroom where I'd been working.

To my relief, she eventually followed me.

Three nights later, as Jamie slept at the control center, her head buried in her arms, I stole away to a time with a comet hurtling through the atmosphere and a lunatic stealing kids away from their beds.

But the comet continued on its way as if my arrival meant nothing, and Joe did, too.

Three

As I'd suspected, my breakthrough caused a stir among the teachers and the council. I was awarded with unlimited access to the Arena and the time travel tech, which I now called the *time manipulator*. I'd been tasked with turning my equations into usable tech. I didn't mention Jamie and I had already done it.

The new freedom was a breath of fresh air. I'd always hated structured learning. I preferred to learn by doing, so tinkering with time travel tech was exhilarating.

I quickly became lost in the process, forgetting the rest of the world existed. Until I heard an uproar in the hallway, that is.

I went into the Arena theater and saw the council enter from the back of the echoing cavern of the auditorium, their faces solemn. Guards followed, dragging Jamie, who screamed as if she was being tortured. She could probably guess what they intended to do with her.

I didn't have a choice. I watched them proceed. My grandmother gave me an almost guilty glance.

"Sky dweller female, you have been found guilty of spying on this village with the intent to disclose information to our enemy. Because of the danger you pose, you have been sentenced to die. We regret the loss of your youth, but we cannot allow you to leave,

16

and you cannot stay here."

I'd never questioned them in all my years of watching the council execute SkyJacks. Now my hands curled into tight balls and my breath came fast. They were going too far. They were crossing lines and taking life when they had no right.

When I'm leader this can't happen, I thought, and I hoped they all heard it.

My grandmother looked at me again. She stood away from the others, her arms across her chest. She opened her mind to me, and I could see she also doubted.

Being a leader means sometimes you make decisions you don't like. We go along for the good of everyone, she silently reminded me.

"You people are the real savages!" Jamie shouted. Her face was pale. "I never had a choice!"

"Please step back into the time stream. There will be no pain. You will simply cease to exist."

Jamie scoffed. "You've tried it yourself?"

I couldn't take another second. If she didn't back into the time stream herself – and SkyJacks never did – a droid would be summoned to push her in. I couldn't let it happen this time.

I stepped forward with all the courage of a future leader and stepped between Jamie and the council members. "She was taken as a child from Manhattan in the 1600's," I said, staring them down with authority I didn't exactly have yet. I added a healthy dose of my sway. They frowned as if they knew what I was doing but were having trouble resisting it. "She's going back to her own time."

Arabella shook her head. "We don't have that technology yet, Morris. Your calculations are promising, but not usable. We don't even have a working prototype to test."

I eyed her with challenge. "Actually, we do."

They were all surprised. I could sense it flowing through the room like a breeze. "It's only been two weeks," one of the men said.

"Turns out Jamie is really good with tech. She helped me build it."

"How can you be sure it works?" he sputtered.

I glanced at Jamie. "We tested it with a squirrel. He survived."

My grandmother's silent voice entered my mind. *You tried it on yourself.*

I didn't look at her, but I answered. *I went back to save Jamie as a child before Joe kidnapped her. I got there too late. It didn't work.*

Her mind wanted to ask questions, but I shook my head. It was a failure I didn't want to revisit.

I'd left the council members speechless. I decided I better lay on my sway thick as molasses for good measure. Their eyes glazed over. I knew I had the advantage.

My grandmother still stared at me, but I ignored her. "I want to try to take Jamie back to her time."

No one spoke. My grandmother nodded as she glanced at the others. "It makes sense."

"The girl is a sky dweller. They aren't to be trusted." The village physician, Christiana Beckett, said. She was afraid I'd talk them into it. "If we make exceptions, they'll destroy us."

"How would they even know, Christiana?" My grandmother shrugged. "If Jamie helped to develop the prototype, she should be taken back to her own time. Thanks to Morris, we have the ability to choose moments of the past now. It's a good thing to right what went wrong. It will bring balance and the advantage could be taken away from the sky dwellers."

One by one, the council members gave their hesitant agreement. I reached for Jamie's hand and led her away from the time stream. Grandmother came to us as the murmuring council left the room.

"You know, I don't remember saying I wanted to go back to my time," Jamie said with a huff.

"Was there somewhere else you wanted to go?" I shot back. "And you're welcome, by the way."

Her eyes narrowed. "I never asked you for anything. I definitely didn't ask you to go back to my childhood and keep me from Joe."

Arabella didn't say it, but I could tell she agreed. "Get Jamie a Transient uniform and spend the rest of the week testing the prototype. I don't want either of you in that manipulator again until we're sure it's safe. You can take her home, but first you have to go somewhere else for me."

Something about her tone made me cringe.

"I knew you would eventually solve the problem of the cylinder speed. Now you'll have to make the necessary changes to the past. You've always been destined to it." Did I detect the smallest measure of uncertainty in my grandmother's voice? Was she second-guessing putting the fate of our people on my shoulders from the time I was a baby?

Too late.

I tried to process all the information she was so calmly piling on me. "So you knew this would happen?"

"You think I've been lying to you your whole life." She noted the direction of my thoughts. "But there's more to it than that, Morris. Everything has to happen in its own time."

I shook my head and tabled my irritation. "So where am I going first?"

"To me," she said. "When I was your age."

I don't know what I was thinking she would say, but it wasn't that. I guess I had hoped maybe she was sending me to my parents. It had been years.

She put her hand on my cheek. "You'll see them again, love."

I fought my emotions. I didn't want to get all weepy about my mom and dad in front of Jamie. I'd seen them once or twice, but the last time I'd been twelve. I'd always told myself the logical truth. They were trying to protect me. The survival of our people depended on the story going the right way. But no matter that it made sense, there was still a big part of me that wanted to be angry at them for abandoning me. And I'd told myself if I ever got to stand in front of them again, I'd ask them why they hadn't found a way for us to stay together.

"See whom?" Jamie, who'd been silently listening to our strange conversation, suddenly spoke.

"Roxy and Levi." I don't know why I hesitated to tell her they were my parents. I was just so used to protecting them from Joe.

She eyed me. "The general has said those names."

I nodded. "Joe wants them dead. And that's why they are hidden – even from me."

"Yes, he hates them and he doesn't mind saying so. But who are they?" Jamie asked again.

"They're my parents," I said with a sigh. "But I haven't seen them in years."

"Morris, can we speak?" Arabella nodded toward the next room, indicating that she wanted to talk to me in private. To Jamie, who rolled her eyes and huffed at us, Arabella indicated the holding cell area. I gave Jamie an apologetic smile as the holding beam was reinitiated.

In the small classroom off the Arena, Arabella put her hands on my arms and squeezed. "I hate to ask this of you on your first mission, but I don't have a choice. It's obvious to me what must happen in the timeline."

I swallowed back a protest, knowing she was right. It wouldn't do any good to argue about it, because it wasn't ultimately her decision, it was mine. Not in my present form, but in some mature future form that had to know better than me. Didn't he? But I hated that my entire life had been planned out for me by future me. I gave her a smile I wasn't feeling. "So where exactly are we headed?"

Her eyes darted to where Jamie waited, watching us with challenge in her expression. I considered her, realizing in that moment I couldn't leave her here, unprotected. I'd come back to find her gone, either by escape or exposure to the time rift.

"She's coming with me." I nodded toward Jamie.

"I don't think that's a good idea."

"I can't leave her here. I can't trust anyone to take care of her."

She sighed, but she didn't argue. "Come back to the house first. I need to show you some things."

She gave Jamie one more glance before she left. As the room went still, it hit me what I was about to do. Up till now, the time manipulator was nothing but a theory. I'd never used it. It was a vision that we knew would be realized, but was only coming true now. It was crazy to think the only thing the past or the future had been waiting on was me – to invent the tech.

I gathered my tools and research before I crossed the hall and turned off the holding beam. I beckoned Jamie with a nod. "Let's go."

She stepped over the threshold without taking her eyes from mine. "Am I allowed to ask where I'm going?"

As if she hadn't just listened to my entire conversation with my grandmother. "I think you've already got that worked out."

"I *think*," she said sarcastically. "That we're going on a trip in a time machine."

"See, you're so smart I don't need to explain anything," I said with a smirk.

As the two of us made our way out of the Arena and up the hill to the shepherd's house, I spent my remaining moments of naivety actually thinking that things were starting to come together for me, even if I didn't have much say in anything. I'd created the time manipulator I'd been nagged about my whole life. I would be free to travel in time and see people I'd been missing. I had a beautiful girl at my side, who possessed a fire in her spirit not unlike my own mother, and who didn't seem to hate me as much as I would have expected a self-respecting SkyJack would. And it might not completely be my gift causing her non-hate, either.

Yes, I decided. Things were looking up.

And, of course, that was the moment everything fell apart.

First, I dropped my box of supplies and notes. They went everywhere, and the Transient village being the frugal place it was, there was not a light to be found save stars and half a moon. I swore and leaned over to pick up the mess.

In the time it took me to stand up, Jamie was gone. She had vanished into the complete darkness of the forest.

I stood up, groaned in absolute frustration and pulled out my laser rifle so I could use the night vision scope. I headed into the woods after her.

It took me a blasted hour to find her. She barely left a track, skittering over obstacles almost like she wasn't held down to the earth by gravity. I'd never even seen a Transient villager with the ability to fly. Could SkyJacks fly?

Nah. Why would they have airships if they could fly?

I finally cornered her when she made the mistake of going up in a tree again. She'd used that tactic before, so I'd been watching the trees carefully with my scope.

"Got you," I said under my breath as I swung up behind her.

She tried to swing to the next tree over, but in the dark she easily missed and took a hard fall on the ground, ripping the Transient prison uniform and probably giving herself quite a few scrapes and bruises she'd be nursing later that night.

It didn't keep her down for long. As I scrambled to grab her, she jumped away from my reach. I managed to get a grasp on her wrist.

"Let me go!" she screamed in rage, pulling so hard I almost lost my grip.

"Stop fighting, Jamie. I'm trying not to hurt you but you're making it hard."

That was when she bit me. Full on, clamped down on my arm with her teeth and bit so hard that blood flowed and trickled down her chin. She didn't let go either, even when I tried to pull away, yelping in pain. It was like a rabid dog had gotten hold of me and wasn't going to release for anything.

Finally I got free, and I could only stand there and whimper as I waited for the blinding pain to stop. When I could think reasonably again, I checked the scope and saw her clambering over a sand hill and disappearing from sight.

I could feel my shirt seeping with blood. I knew I was in for a long night.

Four

In the end, I only found her because she made one fatal mistake. I would always wonder after if she'd done it on purpose. Did she want me to catch her or had she been trapped by my ability?

It was nearing one in the morning when I found her trail. Transient were master trackers, so I saw the slightest imprints of her boot heel around the Collect Pond. I saw her heat signature on my night vision scope as she bent down to fill her water pouch.

I took way more care with my capture the second time. I quickly grabbed her around the waist and lugged her back up to the path. She kicked and screamed and tried to bite the same arm that was still bleeding freely because of her inordinately sharp teeth. I wondered if she'd filed them down.

"Oh, no you don't," I tightened around her arms so she couldn't move from her position. She continued to put up a fight as I dragged her back along the path toward the village.

"Jamie, give it a rest. It's not like I'm going to hurt you. Is it really so important that you get back to the SkyJacks? Is your life there so happy?"

She gradually stopped fighting me, so I cautiously set her down and pointed my laser rifle at her. "Just walk nice and I won't have to use this."

"Go ahead and shoot me." She stared at me darkly. "And I wasn't going back to the SkyJacks. I was heading out on my own."

This surprised me. "You probably wouldn't get too far. You'd get captured by SkyJacks or some other marauding group. America isn't the safest place to wander around these days."

"America?" She said the word curiously, as if she'd never heard it before.

"You've never heard of America? Land of the free, home of the brave? The New World?"

She gave me a blank stare. From the recesses of her mind I heard an echo of a memory she wasn't ready to remember or ready to contemplate.

The New World. New England. New York.

Freedom.

I watched her in all her wild beauty and unrestrained potential. Her determination shone around her in colors of purple, but a white aura I usually associated with goodness appeared in the mist of the darker hues. "You are not all you seem to be, Jamie of the SkyJacks."

"I am your worst nightmare," she promised without missing a beat. "Now, where are we going?"

"If I understand my grandmother correctly, we are going to the past. My family's past. And you're going to check my calculations before we get in that time manipulator so we don't end up swimming in the time stream for the rest of eternity."

"Sounds like a fun way to spend an evening," she quipped, moving along the path toward the Transient village. We traveled in silence for as long as it took to get back to the village, her walking in front of me as I considered her with deeper thoughts than I'd ever considered any other girl before. It bothered me that I'd probably influenced her in order to catch her. I had wanted her to desire that I capture her. I wanted her to want to know me more, like I wanted to know her. I wanted her to have a genuine interest in relationship, because I definitely had one.

I moped as we walked, silent and sullen. My gift was my curse. It had never been good for much of anything except making me feel alienated from everyone. I couldn't even trust my relationship with my grandmother. Sometimes I was sure I was influencing her, and Arabella Eisen was not easily influenced.

"You're quiet," she said with a sniff as we entered the village. She headed toward the imposing Arena, only half-built but intimidating even in its unfinished state. I caught her arm.

"We aren't headed to the Arena."

"Isn't that where your time machine is?"

I smiled. "Officially."

She gave me a strange look but followed me up the hill to the shepherd's house without further comment. I entered the home I'd shared for eighteen years with my grandmother. It had changed from a small, primitive dwelling to the nicest house in the Transient village, with a recycled water system that canceled our need to visit the well every day like the other villagers. Eventually, the plan was for every house to have the water and waste removal systems, but we weren't there yet. We spent more time, effort and resources on protecting our borders and preventing SkyJack attacks than we did on luxuries for our homes.

"This is where you live?" Jamie asked, obvious curiosity coming over her face. I nodded, surveying the simple home through her new perspective and wondering what she thought of it.

"I don't have a home." She folded her hands behind her back and walked into the main room, turning in a complete circle to see everything. "It's simple, but cozy. Like I'd always imagined a home should be." An odd look came over her face. "It reminds me of my home when I was very young."

I nodded. "That doesn't surprise me. It was made to be very simple, like early American homes. Just the basic necessities."

"Morris, I was worried about you," Arabella said, coming

down the stairs with an old notebook in her hand. She had an odd look on her face, one I couldn't decipher even when I tried to read her feelings.

"I had to go after my escaped prisoner," I said, jerking a thumb in Jamie's direction, who smirked proudly.

She stared at the book for a few moments before she handed it to me. "I need you to go back in time. To me, in 2050. I need you to help me build the stabilizing arc for the black hole and solve the time theorem before Leona does."

A little overwhelmed by the information dump, I opened the notebook to the first page to see neat rows of her familiar script. It was a journal.

I'm finally ready to write about what happened to me the day I saw my first specter. As it turns out, it was the day my grandson came from the future to give me the formula for a time machine.

I chuckled in disbelief. I looked up at my grandmother and nodded. "I can help you. This seems pretty straight forward."

"Not everything is as it seems." She was distracted. She paced to the window and held her arms across her chest, hugging herself. "Morris, you're going to see things. You're going to understand some things about me you never knew before."

I nodded, expecting as much. "It's okay, Grandma." I used the less formal nickname I'd called her as a young child. "I know you're not perfect. Nobody is."

She wasn't comforted. Her eyebrows furrowed and she chewed her lip. "I'll let you get to work on your manipulator."

She left us, and a few minutes later I saw her in the field behind our home, staring up at the brilliant night sky. Her worry concerned me more than I was willing to admit.

Five

With Jamie to help me, it didn't take long to finish stabilizing the time manipulator. I discovered her mind was quick and her determination unrelenting. She didn't give up on something she set out to do – ever. I liked that about her. As I worked side by side with her for those few days, I learned more about why she had come to the Transient village in the first place.

"Joe sent me," she admitted. We had been silent and lost in the process of trimming a conversion receptor underneath the small manipulator pad in Shepherd House, and her words came as a surprise. "He sent me to the village to get two things."

I had a feeling I knew what they were. "If I were Joe, I would have sent you to get either our radiation vaccine or our manipulator blueprints."

"He has the blueprints." Jamie said the words without looking up from her laser solder. "He's missing some of the parts."

I sighed. "That *general* of yours is a thorn in our collective side."

"Just because he's as smart as you?"

I sat up and looked at her. "It's not about how smart he is, Jamie, it's about how evil he is. Do you really think he should be able to build a time machine?"

She sat up and shrugged. "If he's smart enough to build one, he will. You just have to decide your next move."

Her words irritated me, so I went back to adjusting connections and fell silent.

"He wanted me to steal the radiation vaccine. And your revive injectors. As many as you had."

"As I would expect. That's why they are guarded by our nastiest droids."

I wondered if it had been a good idea to give her that information.

We finished the secret project in the middle of the night. I woke my grandmother and told her. She sat up with a start and reached for her house jacket.

"Are you sure it's been calibrated correctly?"

"As sure as I can be until we go through it again."

She took a deep breath. "We'll do another test run."

I nodded, agreeing it was a good idea. "Where do you want to send me for the test run?"

"I'm going," Jamie said. I started to argue, but she shot me a look.

"I know where to send you." Grandmother cleared her throat as if she was clearing away all of her doubts and went to the keypad inside the closet. She typed in a number and gestured to the manipulator pad. "Step on."

I got surprisingly nervous as I stepped up to my time manipulator. "What does it feel like?"

She smiled in spite of her nerves. "Like nothing you've ever felt before. If you didn't have those Transient travel suits on, you'd be in for much worse. Nevertheless, it won't be something you soon forget."

I felt Jamie's hand slip into mine as she joined me on the launch pad. I stared at the digital number my grandmother had entered into the computer.

LINEAGE

March 5, 2033, 10:13 a.m.

Then the room turned upside down. My head felt like it was dislodged from the rest of my body and twirled in the air by some teasing cosmic force. Reality bent and shifted as the warm glow of my grandmother's bedroom became the unfathomable blackness of the rift that occurred between the worlds and times connected to each other like a huge rubber band ball. We were snatched from our world and thrown into all of time and space, and my last coherent thought was to hope that 2033 would manage to catch us and put us back on solid ground. I was trusting in my own calculations and experimentation, after all. How could I be sure it was safe?

But Grandmother had told me I'd visited her when she was young. So surely it would work.

Before I could form the words of a grateful prayer, we were standing inside an old building in front of a window overlooking a Manhattan street. I could tell by the tall buildings and incessant traffic we had landed at our destination – 2033. We were standing in the exact place the portal would exist in twenty years or so.

Without a word, I led Jamie down the stairs and out of the old library. We walked down the stone steps to busy 42nd Street. She stood close to me and stared at the lights and movement with fear in her expression.

I didn't blame her. I'd lived my entire life in the Transient village, with the only tech emanating from the portal and reserved for defense rather than convenience. I was overwhelmed by the flashing and the noise. I tried to breathe and focus my calming energy on the area just around us. I felt her grip relax after a few moments.

"Kinda hard to take it all in, huh?" I chuckled, trying not to sound too nervous. "Our city has changed quite a bit in almost two hundred years."

"This is Manhattan?" Her eyes widened as she took it all in. "I can't believe it. I can't believe this used to be here."

"Times change. Things happen. Things like Joe raking a timeship across the city, for one."

She didn't respond to my jab. We stood in silence as the noise pressed in around us. People in strange clothes – bright colors and fabrics of many different styles that revealed more skin than I was used to seeing even from SkyJack girls – brushed past us as if they didn't see us, talking to each other or staring at devices. I recognized some of the tech from the antiques my grandmother had saved. Flat, flexible, transparent devices that they wore as watches or on holsters attached to their arms.

"Who's in charge here?" she asked.

"There is still America, although it's in a fragile place. The people are divided. It will be easy for them to split up the country after the blackout."

The blackout. That was why Grandmother had sent us here. "Jamie, I think this is it. I think this is when the lights go out."

And just as I said the words, a bright light radiated across the entire sky, carrying with it a feeling of intense heat and energy. The sound of a sonic boom accompanied the pops and cracks that began as every one of those devices, along with the vehicles and streetlights and flashing signs hovering above the crowds – went black.

Complete darkness took over the world that had only a moment ago been mesmerized by sound and light.

The sound ceased too – for a moment, anyway. When everyone recovered from their confusion, the screaming began.

I felt Jamie's hand slip into mine as people began to run past us, madly, without direction, as if running from some monster they couldn't see. A large man ran into me, though I could only sense his bulk and smell his sweat. I went careening into the brick wall beside the sidewalk, pulling Jamie along with me.

I felt her pressed against me, heard her soft, panicked

breathing, smelled her sweet scent. "I think it's time to go home. Things are about to get very bad here," I whispered, because there was no need to speak loudly since our faces were an inch apart.

"Okay," she said, but neither of us moved. I reveled in the feel of her. I didn't want to leave the moment, but we had to escape. I knew from the history files that it would only be minutes before mass panic caused the deaths of thousands of Manhattan inhabitants.

I wound my arm around her back to meet the other and hit the control button on my homemade manipulator watch band.

And then I panicked. The screen remained dark.

"Jamie, the EMP killed my control band."

I heard her gasp. She turned around and her fingers traveled lightly down my arm until she found the band. She pressed insistently on the button several times. "We… we have to find an energy source."

"That EMP knocked out every electronic device in the city and most of the rest of the country. A nuclear weapon was detonated into the atmosphere, Jamie. There's no source of power within thousands of miles. It must have not occurred to my grandmother that this would happen."

I felt her mind concentrate hard on an idea. "We need to find a storm."

I gave her a strange look though she couldn't see it. My eyes had begun to adjust to the dark, and I saw the outline of her face as she spoke.

"If we can find an electrical storm, we can jump start the watch. It is powered by the future, so it only needs a second of life to be called back," she yelled close to my ear so I'd hear her over the chaos.

I chuckled. "Turns out you're pretty handy to have on a time travel mission. How do you know all this?"

"Like I said, Joe has all the time travel tech he needs to build a manipulator. He just doesn't have a power source. I've studied this stuff my whole life."

I nodded, thinking. "Okay, if we can find an old vehicle... in this time it would have to be almost sixty years old... we could drive until we come to a storm."

"An automobile without a computer," she acknowledged. "Where are we going to find that?"

"People restored cars for fun before the blackout, even though autopiloted cars were becoming more common in this time. We could find a dealership or an auto shop somewhere, but I don't have my computer to do a search. We need to find a place to safely wait out the night, because it's going to be bad here on the street soon."

She coughed a laugh. "You forget, fragile little Transient villager, you're with a SkyJack. I'll keep you safe."

She held out her knife. "I know how to use it," she assured me.

I couldn't help grinning. "I'm glad for your confidence, but just for my sake, let's hide out in this apartment building tonight. Then tomorrow I say we keep walking down 40th. It will eventually lead to the Lincoln Tunnel. With any luck we'll find someone with a torch to spare. Or a really old car."

Six

We held on to each other and the railing as we climbed the stairs of the apartment. My goal was to get higher than all the people who were coming down and avoid the brunt of the mass panic. We made it to the eighth floor and pushed past the blindly fleeing people. There were several in the hallway with candles, and there was plenty of tension in the air, but having the ability to see kept people in a more reasonable state of mind. We walked down the hallway, trying to blend in. People glanced at our odd clothing with distrustful expressions, but it was Manhattan, after all. No one voiced any objection to us being there.

A wild scream from a child drowned out the murmuring and unease of the adults. I peered around the corner and saw a girl, maybe eight or nine, pulling away from an adult who had a grip on her arm.

"Come, Leona, you'll like living on the farm," the woman said in a high-pitched tone. Another girl about the same age with dark hair stood behind the woman. She watched with large, panicked eyes.

"I won't go! You can't make me!" The redhead shouted, squirming out of the woman's grip.

"I know that girl," I said in surprise.

"Who? The one that's screaming?" Jamie studied the group.

"The quiet one. I think it's my grandmother. Maybe she sent us here to see this."

We listened to the conversation the two women were having. A man stood quietly behind the woman and the second girl.

"The farm is in New Jersey, but it's pretty remote. I think we'll be safe there. As soon as you hear from Michael, join us."

"This whole thing terrifies me, Ashley. And I can't figure out how you both knew this was going to happen."

"It'll be okay, Jenna. Just stay in your apartment and wait for Michael. Lock the doors and pile furniture in front of them. You have all of our food plus your own. You'll be okay until Michael gets to you. Here's the map so you can find us."

The girl with red curls stomped her foot and screeched at the top of her lungs. "I'm not going! No, no, no!"

"Leona, please," Jenna kneeled and took her by the shoulders. "You'll make me very happy if you go with Bella's family and play on the farm with the animals until Mommy and Daddy get there."

"No! I won't!" Her refusal was accompanied by a vicious roar.

I glanced at Jamie. "So... that's my other grandmother."

She raised an eyebrow. "Your other grandmother was a brat. I assume you take after her side?"

Ashley grabbed Leona from the ground and clamped a hand over her mouth. She followed the man, who held a lantern, and the other girl down the hall as little Leona kicked and screamed and bit my great-grandmother's hand until it bled. I gave Jamie a pointed glance and she smirked.

When they got to the stairs at the end of the hallway, the look on Leona's face changed. In a heartbeat, she gave up, and fell against the woman's shoulder with a great sob. I was surprised to see the anguished expression of pure heartbreak.

"She's so young," I said, feeling like I should explain to Jamie. "She's being taken away by strangers. That's got to be scary."

Jamie shrugged. "It happened to me and I didn't throw a fit."

I frowned. "Well, maybe you should have, Jamie. If you had, maybe you wouldn't have been taken."

She seethed. "What do you know, Mr. Transient-Village-all-your-life, never had anything bad happen to you? You have no right to judge me *or* that bratty little kid."

"I was taken away from my parents, too, Jamie."

She was getting ready to come back with another retort, but my words stopped her. "By whom?"

"By me." I chuckled without a lot of humor when I saw the look on her face. "Long story. But I know what it's like to be taken away. Just like you. Just like Leona."

"Sorry." She shrugged.

"Don't worry about it."

We tried to wait out the night in the hallway, but it quickly filled with looters trashing apartments and threatening everyone in their path.

"I think we need to keep moving." I finally stood up and reached for her hand. "It's not any safer here than out on the streets."

Soon enough, people found torches, so we could see the dimly lit activities of panicked New York City. Some fled from cars that were as useless as a pile of scrap metal. I recognized the mental anguish of mothers who had been separated from children and stood screaming for someone to help. We passed people fighting in the doorway of convenience stores as owners attempted to lock their doors and defend their merchandise.

Jamie was fierce. She didn't seem to notice the terror surrounding their beings like an aura of frantic red light. If someone got too close to us, she brandished the knife and growled louder than a bear. I was even scared of her.

We finally got to the edge of the city and saw the water of the Hudson eerily reflecting the torchlight.

Crossing the tunnel was easier said than done. It seemed like everyone else in Manhattan was attempting the same thing. People argued as they pressed against one another.

"Let me through! My kids are home alone!"

"You aren't the only one who has people to find!"

Criminals shamelessly used the situation for their own benefit. One of them reached from behind Jamie to grab her. She savagely roared and lunged at the man. She body slammed him to the cement and when he got back up and came at her again, reaching for her knife, she used it on him. He went down, bleeding and clutching his chest as the crowd trampled over his body.

There was no time to stop and discuss better ways she could have handled the altercation, even though it left a bad taste in my mouth. I grabbed her hand and kept pushing on through the solid wall of people going both ways. I did the best I could to permeate the immediate area with my calming gift. It helped a little, but it was hard to keep it up while we were fighting for our lives.

At least I might keep Jamie from killing anybody else.

We saw an old garage when we came through the other end of the mile-and-a-half long tunnel. I made a bee-line toward it as people spread everywhere and the light from the torches became faint.

It was pitch dark inside the building. "We're going to have to wait until morning." I pulled her inside the building. I wedged a steel beam between the handles and led her to a quiet corner.

She wasn't so keen on waiting. "I'll go out and steal someone's torch," she offered.

I chuckled. "I think it would be safer for everyone if we just wait until dawn. We could use a few hours of sleep anyway. We left the village in the middle of the night."

She sighed loudly to show her disapproval, but I felt her body relax next to me. We stayed close enough for our arms to touch.

Her warmth comforted me. I wasn't alone in this strange place in the past.

"I'm glad you're here, Jamie," was the last thing I said before I went to sleep.

She didn't answer, but I suspected she was glad, too.

When I opened my eyes again, it was daylight. Someone pounded relentlessly on the door, screaming for help.

I went to the window in the stairwell and looked down. A man tried to open the door as another man beat him to the ground. I started to run down the stairs, but the man crumpled on the ground in a pool of blood from the attacker's knife. It was obvious he wouldn't be getting back up.

I went back to Jamie. "Let's see if we can find a car in here somewhere. I'm ready to leave 2033."

"Me too." She came to the window and looked down at the grisly scene. She didn't wince or make any noise that I would have expected of a teenage girl. She just stared thoughtfully as if she was piecing together what had happened.

"Do you think your grandmother knew the EMP would knock out your timeband?"

I shook my head. "Maybe she didn't think of it. Maybe she thought I needed this test before I began my duty fixing time."

Jamie glanced at me, her gaze incredulous.

"I don't expect you to understand everything. I don't understand everything myself. But my grandmother knows what she's doing, and I trust her."

Jamie shrugged.

I went through the garage, opening doors and examining all the vehicles. It was jolting to see so many antiques in their new state, and part of me wanted to spend some time looking at them, but I knew we needed to move. I saw our prize in the back of the store, hidden behind the others as if someone was saving it just for themselves. It had been newly restored and detailed.

"It's a Firebird," I said in awe. "I've never seen one in this condition."

"Is it old enough?" She came from the other side of the garage as she answered.

"Yes. This is the model released in 1967, if I remember my History of Mechanics correctly. As long as they didn't rebuild the engine and add electronic components, this should work."

While I worked on manually opening the electric-powered garage door, Jamie scrounged around in the office for a few minutes until she found the right key. I pried open the door before I returned to the car. As I slipped inside the door and felt the cool leather seats, I got a thrill of anticipation. It looked untouched. It might work. I noticed a small white card stuck to the bottom of the dashboard.

I knew the EMP would ground you. I took care of saving this car right out of the 1967 factory. Just remember at some point in your travels to leave it where you'll find it. Love you! Grandma

I chuckled. Jamie got in the other side and handed me the key. She looked a little miffed that I was driving, but I distracted her by showing her the note.

I turned the key and hoped for the best. The engine roared to life.

She laughed out loud and slapped the dashboard as I revved the engine and tried to remember what to do next.

"Why aren't we going?" She pushed my arm. I was embarrassed to tell her I didn't know how to drive a car.

"We don't have cars in the village," I reminded her in a defensive tone.

She held her hands up in the air. "It doesn't look that hard. I drive airships all the time. Let me drive!"

I frowned at her and put my foot on the brake pedal. At least I was pretty sure it was the brake pedal. It didn't go anywhere, at

39

least.

"I think you pull on this," Jamie tapped a lever that came up out of the floor in the middle.

"I knew that." I pulled on it until it went to the "D" position. I hoped that meant "drive." I didn't tell her I was relieved Grandma had left me an automatic.

The car lurched forward, roaring as if to protest my ignorance as its driver. I slammed on the brakes, but it didn't take me long to figure out how to smoothly drive forward and out of the garage.

There was no top on the car and it was March. Jamie shivered in her Transient prison uniform. I thought about keeping her warm, but the console came between our leather seats. I wasn't sure she'd be up for it, anyway, and I didn't want to be bitten again.

We rode in silence since the car noise was so loud. I tried to make sense of the roads. I eventually found an old highway that led northwest out of the city, so I just kept driving until we had escaped the crazy tangle of streets and buildings and approached scenes more rural and peaceful.

We used up almost the whole tank of gas before we came upon a storm squall. When we were right underneath the cell, I stopped the car and we ran up to the top of a hill as the rain streamed down our cheeks and soaked our hair and clothes. I hoped our haphazard plan might actually work.

"There!" Jamie pointed up at the sky. I stared in wonder at the odd sight. Two rainbows were cast from some sort of prism-like instrument at the top of the hill. We jogged up to it and I looked it over. It was Transient tech, but I'd never seen it before.

"I think it's our power source," she said.

Jamie took my time watch and used a large, flat rock next to the prism as her table. She opened up the back and rearranged the circuits with delicate precision.

I kept stealing glances at her face as she worked. Jamie was smart. Really smart. I wondered what this girl could accomplish for the village. Maybe she could even get the droid program organized. We'd been trying to get an army of droids together, but the work was tedious and the technology wasn't coming together as fast as we wanted.

As I mused, lightning suddenly shot out of the sky and hit the rock, attracted to whatever beacon she'd set up.

"I don't think this ride is going to be quite as smooth as the first one," she warned as she slapped the newly charged watch back on my arm and put her arms around my waist. She held me tight as another burst of electricity hit the prism.

It didn't take long. One moment we were standing in the rain and I was holding the softest, prettiest girl I'd ever held as close as I possibly could; another moment we were hurtling through time and space, stretched and compacted and gasping for air as everything moved faster than light, yet in slow motion.

An eternity and a moment later, we fell onto the floor in my grandmother's closet.

"I'd say you've been through the ringer," Arabella said with an amused expression as she surveyed our torn, soaked clothes.

"A little warning that you were sending us to the blackout would have been nice," I complained.

"At least I got you a car. And a power source."

"If you wanted to do a test, why not send us one minute into the past?" I wasn't done complaining.

She shrugged. "I assume that's the first test you did when you finished your prototype."

She was right, but I didn't want to admit it.

"There are tests for tech, and then there are tests for people. You needed to understand what happened at the very beginning." She smiled, but I saw a hint of uncertainty behind her eyes. Did she ever second guess her decisions?

Her eyes met mine. "All the time, Morris."

I offered a short nod, which made Jamie frown. In that moment I realized my grandmother didn't have everything figured out. In a strange way it gave me comfort. Sometimes you just did the best you could and went with your gut feeling.

Arabella's voice interrupted my thought. "Get changed. I've got a meal waiting for you downstairs. Then you're off to 2050."

"Oh, great," Jamie said with sarcasm.

Seven

After some food and a change of clothes, my grandmother unceremoniously handed me a journal of hand-written notes. "I started writing this around the time of the blackout. It documents the Second Civil War and how Leona's parents and my father died in the Battle for New York City, how the United States split and how we finally regained power. I also kept a diary of everything that happened after Leona and I went to Princeton. Any questions you have should be in there, including the formula for the portal and the wormhole."

"It kind of takes the fun out of it, knowing you didn't come up with this yourself," I said. "Not to mention it's a paradox because this formula really doesn't come from anywhere."

"The true genius is Leona. She came up with it herself. But her intentions are not as future-focused as we need them to be. Besides, since when are you, of all people, scared of paradoxes?" She raised an eyebrow at me. Jamie gave me a questioning look

I explained. "I was born in 1776 to parents who were born in the 2050's." I shrugged. "And if that's not weird enough, my older self came and took me as a baby from that time to my grandmother in 2077 to keep me safe."

"You took yourself through time?" Jamie laughed like I was

a freak.

I huffed defensively. "Actually, I haven't yet, technically."

"Don't worry, I won't tell anyone," she said with another snicker. "I never expected you to be as cool as a SkyJack."

That reminded me. "Gram, I think you should talk to the council. Jamie might be able to do something to get our droid defense army up and running."

Arabella was interested. "What makes you think that?"

"She's a wiz with this stuff, it turns out."

"A wiz, huh?" Arabella raised an eyebrow, sizing Jamie up. "And just what would you do to improve our droids? They need more common sense than they currently have. They don't seem to recognize the difference between friend or foe. We can only use them as guard dogs, so to speak, because they'd just as easily turn on us."

Jamie considered the question as Arabella brought up a plan of the current robot in production at the Arena. She flipped through the 7-D model and changed a few circuits and equations with lightning speed.

"They need a bio-mechanical element." Jamie closed the digital enhancement with a finality that told us she was absolutely sure of her diagnosis.

I laughed before I realized she was serious.

"You mean put something living in them?" I exchanged an uneasy glance with my grandmother. Maybe Jamie wasn't the best candidate to win over the council after all.

She shrugged with indifference. "Not necessarily. It wouldn't have to be presently living. Just recently. And it would have to be human. What do you do with the SkyJack bodies after a battle? Or what do you do with your own dead, for that matter?"

A long, awkward silence filled the space. My grandmother cleared her throat and entered the destination into the new portal control I'd created. I saw she'd already made a few adjustments.

"I'm going with your term—the *time manipulator*," she

explained. "Since we can manipulate it."

"Makes sense, doesn't it?" I said with a grin. "Jamie, let's go save the past."

Jamie stalked to the pad inside the closet, leaving room for me to join her.

"What happened to your arm?" Arabella stopped me as I passed her. I looked down at the makeshift bandage I had on the bite Jamie had given me.

"One of those crazy SkyJacks bit me." I shot a glare Jamie's way. "Can you believe it?"

She frowned. "I wish Levi were here to heal it for you. It will be nice when Physician Beckett discovers how to give us all healing abilities."

I couldn't argue with that.

She fussed with the bandage. "I hope you cleaned it well. You never know where those teeth have been."

I huffed. "Got that right."

"I'm sure you'll live, princess," Jamie said, crossing her arms. "Are we going or not?"

I hopped up on the pad. "Let's go."

The manipulator burst to life and seconds later we were riding the winding loops of time with only a wormhole to keep us from flying out of the rift.

We landed more efficiently and neatly in 2050 than we had for the blackout. I was convinced that Arabella had improved on my design. We were still standing when we landed, and we were facing the library instead of in it.

"Wow, check out this building!" I was in awe. "It looks like they added several floors since 2033, maybe for the researchers to work in."

The base of the Public Library built in the early 1900's still stood, but there were several layers on top of it. They fit seamlessly and towered above the street. I looked down 2050's Fifth Avenue. It contained an odd mixture of animals and carts and modern cars. The cars were small and sleek and the first of the successful solar-powered technology that would soon have the mag-lev function of my parents' New York.

"It looks like they can't make up their mind whether they're modern or in the past," Jamie said as she turned in a circle to appreciate all the sights.

"It's because of the blackout. It caused quite a wide divide between the rich and poor. When electricity was restored, it was expensive and only available to the rich, who were also in control of rebuilding and employment. You either lived in luxury or you served in relative poverty."

"What did your grandmothers do?" Jamie asked curiously.

"They were fortunate to be geniuses," I said with a smile. "They were both picked after college to become part of the team that would live in the upstairs floors of the library. They built a device that would control the effect of the black hole that started pulling on Earth."

"Your grandmas saved the world?" Jamie said in a tone, either impressed or sarcastic, I couldn't tell which.

"Pretty much. Although if you think about it, I guess we could make a case for us saving it since we're here with the formula."

"Yeah, tell me again why we shouldn't let Leona solve this on her own? Seems to me the less you mess with the past the lower the chance you'll affect your own destiny."

I nodded. "That's our philosophy. But we've also come to understand certain events were helped along in the first place, and we have reason to believe nothing will happen the way it should if we don't interfere," I explained. "I've been prepped my entire life for this purpose. To go back and fix what went wrong, or what would have gone wrong if I hadn't. It's pretty much my fate."

"Sounds like a rough fate to me." She walked toward the library, still hugging her chest with her long, slender arms. I stood for a moment and watched her, mesmerized.

She turned around and narrowed her eyes. "Don't be using

that voodoo on me, Morris Koenig."

I shook my head, trying to wake up from where my thoughts were going. "Was I doing it?"

For a moment, her eyes showed confusion. Then she replaced it with a cool indifference. "I told you before; no magic. You wanna get to me, you better do it the old-fashioned way."

I couldn't help grinning at her statement. "So you're saying there's a chance?"

She scoffed. "Hardly. You can't help yourself. You just think every girl will fall over you every time you stand close. You're lazy, Morris. I have no interest in lazy Transient royalty who care more about people who've been dead for fifty years than any real relationship."

She walked toward the library, apparently done talking about it. I followed, but I couldn't get the stupid grin off my face.

"I take that to mean there's a chance."

Eight

Getting into the library would have been harder – or easier, depending on perspective – if I didn't have a SkyJack on hand. I was going to walk up to the security detail standing around the perimeter with long, scary guns and explain that my grandmother was inside and I needed to speak to her. I was hoping they'd message her and she'd be curious enough to get me in.

Jamie had a different idea.

I cleared my throat and approached the young woman in army camo staring me down like I'd already committed a shootable offense by coming too close. She held the gun rigidly across her body and lifted it an inch in warning.

"Excuse me, I'm really sorry to bother you," I gave her my most winning smile and laid on the charm with my gift. I wasn't too worried. Usually, my calming influence went a long way in priming people to be helpful.

Her face had relaxed and her gun had gone slack by the time I was within a couple feet of her. She didn't smile, but she appeared expectant, waiting for me to talk.

"My gran – that is, my sister works here, and I really need to talk to her about a family emergency. Any chance you can let me in?"

She started to shake her head, uncertainly enough for me to suspect I could talk her into it.

Until I realized Jamie was no longer standing beside me. I turned around and gawked in surprise as she reached into the bushes and raked her fingers through the mud. She stood up and drew dark circles around her eyes with the dirt. Then she stared at the soldier with an expression reminiscent of a bull in a field getting ready to take on a challenger.

Then she screamed. Not a high-pitched, frightened scream, but a terrifyingly wild shriek that made every person on the terrace and steps turn and watch.

Jamie ran toward the female guard, and before she could react, Jamie was holding her gun and pointing it at her head. Instead of shooting her, Jamie turned it sideways and rushed at the soldier, expertly using the weapon as a baton to whack the girl in the back and rake it under her feet. She landed on top of the unfortunate guard and held the gun across her neck.

"Let. Us. In."

It was more of a growl than a voice. The guard stared as if not sure whether to laugh or cry, then wordlessly handed me a transparent key pass.

"I was going to let him in," the guard said to Jamie.

Jamie didn't seem embarrassed. She jumped off the guard but left the gun on her neck, unconcerned. I followed her up to the door where I scanned the pass as I looked at her out of the corner of my eye. I wasn't exactly sure I shouldn't run for my life.

She raised an eyebrow. "Stop staring, Koenig. Haven't you ever seen a SkyJack do her thing before?"

She had me there. She was, in fact, acting exactly as SkyJacks behaved. I didn't answer.

A pleasant voice spoke from a hologram above the door. "Welcome, citizen. Please state your name and business. You are being recorded and observed from every direction, so please do not attempt to break any of our city's laws."

49

She spoke with such a cheerful voice. I could hardly be offended that she thought we were criminals. "Uh, I need to speak to my *sister*." I emphasized the word. The computer generated image wouldn't get it, but if Arabella was listening, she might pick up on it. "My name is Morris Koenig."

"Division and ID reference number?"

"Uh, well, I'm not sure," I fumbled. "She is a scientist. She works on the black hole project –"

The doors immediately shot open. As I stepped over the threshold, guards surrounded us and whisked us out of the main foyer.

We were brought into a small office where a severe woman glared at us over her geometric glasses. I tried not to laugh at the silly design that must be the trend among the upper class.

"What in the world made you think those spectacles were attractive?" Jamie curled her lip in disgust.

The woman's eyes narrowed. "This from the girl with dirt around her eyes and hair that looks like sun-parched straw."

"I wasn't going for fashionable." Jamie shrugged.

The woman looked at me. "What do you mean by attacking the sentry and trying to force your way into this building? Only those in the upper class are allowed in the library."

"This is a public library. It's supposed to be open to everyone." I shook my head in disbelief.

She scoffed. "Have you been out of touch with reality for the past twenty years? There are no free places to under-laborers. You don't have the look of uppers to me."

I smiled, taking a deep breath and letting my gift out of its box. The air permeated with the vibe. "Please don't be alarmed. My friend is upper, but she has gone insane. She was kidnapped by marauders outside the city and she hasn't gotten better like we'd hoped. I need to see my sister and ask her advice about which sanctuary would be best."

"Your sister?" The woman's face had mellowed. Jamie wisely

kept her mouth shut, though I felt her disgust directed at me.

I almost said "Arabella Eisen," but at the last minute I changed my mind. "Leona Koenig."

"I didn't know Doctor Koenig had a brother." The woman was suspicious, but she couldn't help the easy smile that spread over her features. My ability had done the trick. I returned the smile and stepped closer, leaning over her desk.

"She doesn't like to admit to my existence. You know how sisters are. If you call up to her, I'm sure she'll be willing to see me. My name is Morris Koenig."

"Hmm." She didn't sound convinced, but she pressed the communicator module on her desk. "Get me Dr. Koenig."

A moment later, the clear, young voice of my grandmother Leona spoke. "Yes?"

"Dr. Koenig, so sorry to bother, but I have a young man here who claims to be your brother. His name is Morris Koenig."

There was a long pause. I held my breath. Jamie leaned close to my ear. "Are you ready to do this my way?" she whispered.

I frowned at her as Leona finally spoke again.

"Send him up."

I breathed a sigh of relief. I tried not to think too hard about meeting my grandmother who would soon take over the city by threatening to kill everyone in her portal.

"You realize we're going to meet a crazy person right now, don't you?" Jamie crossed her arms over her chest as the woman led us to a high-tech transparent elevator.

"Sector 5, theoretical science." The woman spoke to the computer and directed us inside. I turned to Jamie as the door whisked shut and we were efficiently carried away on some sort of hydraulic system connected to the mainframe computer.

"*She's* a crazy person? I'd think she'd make you good company."

I meant the words as a joke, but it surprised me that she seemed upset. She huffed and turned the other way, but I could easily read her emotions. She was hurt.

"I'm sorry," I mumbled before the elevator came to a stop and the door opened.

I stepped out into a sterile white hallway. The lighting was soft and animated pictures of scientists were the only decoration apart from the pale atmosphere.

No one met us in the hallway, so we tiptoed along, checking the digital title for each room until we found the one we were looking for.

"Koenig and Eisen, theoretical science, mission Noah's Ark."

"Noah's Ark?" Jamie asked.

"The ancient story about how God destroyed the world with a flood, but saved one family with an ark. A big boat." I wasn't surprised she'd never heard of it. Joe probably didn't tell his assassins many Bible stories.

"Oh," she nodded, giving me an odd look I wasn't sure how to read.

The door to their lab was open, but no one stood there waiting for us. I could hear two voices in the back of the room, arguing. I stepped inside, followed by Jamie, and quietly followed the sound.

"It's not ready yet, Lee." My grandmother's voice was higher, clearer, but it was her voice I knew and loved. "I didn't mean for anyone to take it until I tested it more."

"The sooner we take it, the sooner we can start building the portal," Leona argued in an authoritative voice. "This is no time to play it safe and you know it."

"Just give me a few more months and let me test it."

"No!"

I heard the sound of scuffling and turned the corner to see a young, beautiful Leona grab a syringe away from an equally lovely Arabella.

Leona jabbed the needle into her leg and quickly dispensed the blue liquid into her skin.

"That was risky," Arabella chastised. But she took another

syringe from the holder and injected herself. Leona just smiled.

"Soon we'll rule the world, Bell. You and I." Leona grabbed Arabella's hands and squeezed them in excitement. "We all but have the formula. No one can stop us. We'll save the world, and they'll make us queens out of gratitude."

"I don't want to be a queen," Arabella said, uncomfortable. "I just want everyone to be okay."

"Oh, don't pretend to be modest," Leona scoffed. She let go of her hands and danced around the room until she came to a large transparent board full of scientific equations. Beyond it, I recognized the skeletal beginnings of the portal. "I'm so close. I'm going to find the answer. Tonight."

"I don't feel very well." Arabella did indeed look pale.

"That's the problem with you, Bell," Leona said, rolling her eyes. "You never were very strong."

I cleared my throat and both women turned to look at Jamie and me. Arabella met my eyes with a sort of recognition that confused her, while Leona looked us up and down with all the distrust of a future oppressor.

"So you're the one who claims to be Morris Koenig. What are you up to?"

I stepped forward. "I *am* Morris Koenig. And this is Jamie Salvatore. I'm here to see Arabella Eisen."

Her eyes widened. "Me?"

"Where are you from? Who sent you?" Leona demanded. I noticed she'd begun to sweat and her eyes were glassy, probably from the injection.

"You sent me." I looked straight into Arabella's eyes. "I'm from the future. 2094."

Leona loudly scoffed as Arabella took a step back.

"And just what sort of proof do you have of that claim?" Leona huffed.

"Listen, lady, how about you sit down and shut up and let him explain?" Jamie leaned forward.

"How about you find out what my laser gun can do to your pretty little face?" Leona reached to the table for her gun.

I held up my hands and took a deep breath, using my calm to quiet both of them. Arabella watched me with interest and took a step closer.

"What did you just do?"

I nodded, glad she had recognized it. "I used my gift."

"Your gift?"

I nodded toward the empty syringes on the table. "You gave me your radiation vaccine when I was a baby. It protected me from radiation, but it did something else. You're probably going to figure that out pretty quickly. Maybe in the next few minutes."

Leona was interested. "Gifts? What do you mean?"

"You don't realize it yet, of course, but the radiation vaccine awakens gifts. Supernatural abilities somewhat based in the individual's personality. I have the gift of calm. I can help others feel more relaxed and at peace if I am standing close to them. They feel happy."

"It doesn't work on me," Leona decided. She wiped her damp brow and started to breathe more heavily. She looked at Jamie. "So what gift do you have?"

"I have the gift of kicking the crap out of people," Jamie answered immediately.

"She doesn't have a gift. She was never vaccinated," I explained quickly, hoping to avoid an altercation. Having Jamie and Leona in the same room was like carrying a torch into a chamber full of dynamite.

Jamie shot a look at me, assuring me I'd said the wrong thing. She raised an eyebrow and pinched her lips together tightly as she stepped to the table and took another syringe from the tester. She stabbed herself in the leg before I could stop her.

"Jamie!" I was going to go into a list of all the reasons why she shouldn't have done that and would probably die as a result, but she didn't look the least bit sorry, so I waved her off. I turned back to Arabella.

"Since I got it when I was a baby, I'm not sure how adults react to it. I think you both might be experiencing a little radiation sickness from the dose of subatomic particles contained in the vaccine." I shot Jamie a look. "You have *that* to look forward to."

"Even if I did feel sick I wouldn't tell you." Jamie sniffed.

"I had hoped I didn't use enough to make us sick, but that was why I wanted to test it before we used it on ourselves," Arabella said quietly, covering her abdomen with her arms. "I'm feeling a little sick to my stomach."

I helped her sit down. She didn't smile, but I felt her relax.

"My parents both have gifts as well. My dad is a healer and my mom can read minds," I told her.

She hesitated. "Who are your parents?"

I smiled. "I don't want to give you any spoilers. I'll just leave it at that. But I have something I'd like to show you in private."

Leona reacted. "Whatever you have to show her you can show me. We are best friends, and we've never kept anything from each other. We share *everything*."

Arabella smiled weakly at me. "It's okay. We don't keep secrets."

I resisted the urge to scoff aloud. "Just the same, I need to stick to my mission. This is for your eyes only."

Nine

Arabella exchanged a glance with Leona, but she got up and followed me out of the room.

"I don't think we should leave those two alone very long, but I've been sent here to show you this journal." I pulled it out of the small, portal-proof bag I wore around my chest and handed it to her.

"I don't believe it," she whispered, hesitantly reaching for the old journal with yellowed pages and worn away leather. "I have this journal. Leona gave it to me for my birthday just last month. But I haven't written in it yet."

My young grandmother opened it with shaky hands. She ran her fingers across the yellowed pages and nodded. "I suppose it's wise to use paper. Digital journals could be lost, as in the blackout."

I glanced into the lab to see if Jamie and Leona had killed each other yet. They were arguing about something.

Arabella read the first entry. "*I'm finally ready to write about what happened to me the day I saw my first specter. As it turns out, it was the day my grandson came from the future to give me the formula for a time machine.*"

Her hands trembled so much she almost dropped the book. She kept her eyes fastened on the page as she spoke. "Grandson?"

"I'm your grandson. The son of your daughter and Leona's son."

I shouldn't have told her so much. She dropped the journal and covered her mouth with her hands, tears appearing in her eyes. I was about to apologize, but she came near and put her hands on my cheeks. "I knew you were family the moment you stepped into the room."

I nodded and smiled, covering her hands with mine and feeling pretty emotional as I looked into her familiar brown eyes.

She dropped her hands and reached for the book on the floor. "So if you are here now, I suppose I have my proof that your time travel theorem is real."

"It is."

"But why give it to me? Leona has all but solved it already. And is it wise to return to the past and give your secrets? You may change things."

I nodded. "All of this has been taken into account at our village in the future."

"Village?" She chuckled in disbelief. "In Manhattan?"

I followed her gaze out the window and surveyed the city, jam packed with buildings as high and far as the eye could fathom. No space for a village presented itself for consideration.

"The Manhattan of the future is very different. But you will see for yourself one day. For now, these are the things you have recorded for your younger self. There are reasons for everything. You *must* solve the time formula before Leona does."

"But she's my best friend." Arabella's voice faltered. "I don't want to hurt her. She's worked so hard."

I wasn't sure how to explain to her that her best friend would soon take possession of the portal and the city, kill Arabella's husband and send her infant daughter into hiding. I pointed to the journal. "You have the answers. Trust yourself."

She gave me a look that said she wasn't so sure that was a wise idea, but she found her place and began to read out loud. I could see the words in her writing without looking at them by closing my eyes and seeing through her mind.

Remembering the specter is like remembering a nightmare that once troubled my sleep, rather than recalling something from reality. But it was real. I looked into its haunting blank eyes as it stared at me. Through me, really. Such a mournful stare I've never seen before or since.

It came to me in the portal testing room, late in the night after my grandson gave me this journal. I returned it to him and never looked at it again. What I write, I imagine pens itself onto the paper of the other journal.

I felt like a traitor when I stared at Leona's sleeping form. She'd fallen asleep exhausted, sick from the vaccine, right in front of her precious board where she was one equation away from solving the problem that would fix the entire world.

And I stepped in and solved it for her. Not because I'd figured it out, but because I'd been given the information. I cheated, and I fear that it will change everything.

When I entered the equation into the portal receptor we'd already created, the lights went out in the entire building and most of the surrounding area of Manhattan. I was afraid at first that I'd caused another blackout. But they came back on a moment later, so bright I couldn't see a thing for a few minutes. The portal came alive. If the doors hadn't been shut or hadn't been strong enough to hold in the blast of suction from the black hole, we'd have all been sent to oblivion.

Leona stood up and screamed. Not because she was scared or hurt, but because she was mad. Entirely, utterly angry at me for solving it behind her back. She flew at me and knocked me over, and

that's when we saw the specter. He stood over us as if he expected us to solve whatever had gone wrong with him, too. His brows furrowed over dark circles where his eyes should have been, and his skeletal form reached toward us. He was human, but he wasn't. His skin was white, his hands like leather. But his legs and feet were machines, elevating him so far above the ground I wanted to scream in terror
. . .

Arabella snapped shut the book and dropped it back into my hand as if it were a hot coal. "That's enough." She shook her head. "I don't need to know anymore. I know what I have to do."

I nodded, wondering about the specter she had mentioned. It didn't sound familiar to me. Was it from my future? It kind of sounded like the biodroid Jamie wanted to build.

Arabella's face had gone pale and she stumbled as if she was dizzy. I remembered she was dealing with the vaccination side effects on top of everything else. I wanted to tell her to rest and deal with it all when she felt better, but I knew that wasn't how it was supposed to go. She'd have to push through the effects of the vaccine if she was going to save the world before Leona.

"One thing I don't understand, Morris," she said weakly. "Why can't Leona solve this?"

"Leona's future is not what you would have wanted for her. She's about to make some very bad decisions. And if she solves the problem of time travel, she will be the only one who understands how it works. You have to solve it first so we can have the advantage when she tries to destroy her people with it."

Arabella's entire body seemed to sigh, though she didn't exactly seem surprised. "I was afraid of that. I've always been afraid of that."

"With good reason," I said, not sure what else to say.

A frustrated cry saved us from any more conversation.

I ran into the next room where Leona's piercing expression trained on Jamie with all the concentration of someone experimenting with their powers. Jamie was splayed on the floor, contorting to odd angles as she cried out in anguish.

"She's doing it," Jamie forced the words out with a low groan.

I ran at Leona and knocked her over, breaking her connection with Jamie. Fortunately, she wasn't experienced enough with her power to turn it on me, so I used my own ability to calm her down.

Leona chuckled, unconcerned that Jamie was still rolling back and forth on the floor in pain. "Did you see that, Bell? Did you see what I could do?"

"Leona, you hurt her," Arabella said, kneeling and helping Jamie sit up. "Why would you do that?"

Leona frowned, as if she hadn't considered why and she didn't think it was important. "Because I could."

Arabella didn't challenge her, but exchanged a look with me and a small nod that told me she saw my point.

Leona looked exhausted and she sunk into a chair. "Wow. That took a lot out of me. I guess it must use lots of energy. I feel like I just ran a marathon."

"Why don't you rest a while?" Arabella suggested with a falsely friendly tone.

Leona nodded. "Good idea. When I wake up, I'll solve the equation, and we'll save the world, Bell."

"Sure, Lee. Sounds good." Arabella deposited Jamie on my arm and went to get Leona a pillow from the white cabinet on the far wall. Leona curled up in front of her transparent board and fell asleep.

Arabella grimaced. "I need to go to my rooms."

"Sure." I nodded, turning my attention to Jamie. I ran my hand over her cheek. "Are you okay?"

She stopped leaning on me and stood up. "I think so. It felt like she was torturing me from the inside. With her mind."

"Yeah." I wasn't surprised. "She does that."

"No wonder she'll take over the city."

"You look sick," I said, worried. Her lips were white and her eyes wouldn't stay open.

"I am." She rubbed her eyes and tried to sit up. "Either she is really good at her torture already or I'm sick from the vaccine."

"You shouldn't have given yourself that injection." I was worried. Really worried. It was one thing for Arabella and Leona. They had taken it fifty years ago and been fine. Jamie was another story. Who knew how she'd react to it?

"Let me go." She stubbornly pushed my hands away and stood up. "I'm fine."

"Yeah, right. I need to get you out of here."

"Stop hovering."

Arabella returned, going to Leona and leaning down beside her. Her face contorted with sorrow. "Everything changes today, doesn't it?"

I didn't want to tell her, but I didn't see a way around it. I nodded.

She sat for a long time. She reached over and smoothed the strawberry blonde curls that framed Leona's sleeping face like a halo. "It started when she lost her parents – her obsession with control. She's so determined and so smart… I wanted her gifts to be used for good in such a time as this, when people need strong leaders. I had so hoped…"

She sighed, and I caught a glimpse of my grandmother in the future. Her long brown hair and chocolate eyes complimented her in a way Leona's striking beauty couldn't. To look into Arabella's face was to know peace. Even at her younger age.

She gave me a weary smile. "I need to message Eli, my fiancé. When I get back, I'll complete the theorem."

Ten

Arabella gave us the pass code to her apartment on the upper floor of the library. Then she pulled her long brown hair into a ponytail as she turned toward the transparent board. She erased a portion of the equations at the bottom where she would complete the necessary work. I helped Jamie toward the door. She'd become very weak in the minutes that followed our conversation, and I was getting worried.

"Morris," Arabella called without looking back. "My apartment is set to report a break-in if someone without my DNA opens them unauthorized. Fair warning."

I chuckled. "No problem."

She looked at me, and a wide smile – the one I was used to back at home – spread across her face. "I guess you really are family."

"I am." I nodded.

"It gives me hope, you know," she said, pulling a comfortable-looking old sweater around her shoulders. I noticed her hands were still shaking. "To know that even if she does what you say she'll do," she nodded at Leona, "our children will have a child together. You may think you shouldn't have told me that, but I needed to know to get through this."

"I promise you everything will happen the way it's supposed to happen. I will see to it."

She nodded at my solemn words. "I look forward to meeting my daughter. What is she like?"

I felt the sadness pull at my smile and my eyes stung. "She's great. Amazing. I miss her."

Too late, I realized I shouldn't have said so much. Her expression clouded. "What do you mean? You can't be more than eighteen. Is she gone already?"

I shook my head. "Not gone. Just in a different time zone."

She frowned, and I could see she wasn't satisfied by my vague answer. But I turned away from her and left the lab before she could ask any more questions.

I missed my parents. More than anything, I wanted to see them.

I watched Jamie sleep on the lavish couch in a stylish set of luxury rooms with design trends and upgrades I'd never seen before, let alone imagined. As I did, I slipped into a funk. I eyed the grandeur morosely, knowing full well there was a city of struggling poor trying to survive in the streets below. How did my grandmother live in a place like this and keep her humility? Leona certainly hadn't.

"It's not fair," I whispered. My eyes fell to the timeband on my wrist.

It was the first time it really occurred to me that I had solved the problem of time specific travel, and now had a time manipulator at my disposal. What was stopping me from visiting my parents?

The answer was easy enough. I didn't know where they were.

I eventually fell asleep, lulled by the soft, cool sound of air blowing far above in the steel chute that ran across the ceiling. But even my unconscious mind was aware that Arabella was seeing worlds beyond my own and changing them as I slept.

I woke early, not sure what had caused me to open my eyes. Jamie still slept fitfully, a troubled expression on her face. She made sounds in her sleep that made me smile. She sounded a bit like a bear cub growling at a playmate.

Suddenly, I felt the fight that had started.

I didn't hear the yelling with my ears, but I sensed it like a whack on the head. It felt like it had the one time my grandmother had become very angry with a Transient defector who was found to be spying for Joe. They had been friends, and she had taken the betrayal hard. I had felt her emotions then, and now I felt them again. Only I didn't think it was Arabella this time. The anger felt more unstable. That could only mean one person was responsible.

I ran back to the lab to find the door open and a young man standing near it, holding up his hands. "Calm down, Leona. Why don't you sit? You look ill."

Leona only raged louder. "How could you, you ugly, backstabbing traitor!"

Arabella began to writhe in agony. "Leona... please..."

"What's happening? Arabella?" The man in the doorway, whom I assumed was my grandfather, Eli, ran to her side and lifted her into his arms to try to keep her from hurting herself. Leona stood over them, staring at Arabella with deadly intent.

"Stop it!" I yelled at Leona, hoping to deflect her attention to me. "You'll kill her!"

"She isn't doing anything," Eli said, his voice faltering like he wasn't sure he wanted to hear what he was missing.

"She's trying to kill her. Leona, cut it out or she'll die! You won't get anything you want that way."

My plan worked and Leona's piercing gaze found mine. "Why should I listen to you? I don't even know who you are or how you got in here. For all I know, you're the one that gave her the formula to steal everything away from me. You deserve what you get!"

I felt the pain then. It shot through me like lightning, making me feel like I would split apart at the atomic level. I couldn't help the groans that erupted from within.

"Morris!" Jamie came through the door, staring in surprise at what was happening. Then something really strange happened, weirder than the already odd scenario of my grandmother trying to kill me with her death-ray, tractor-beam eyes.

A laser rifle appeared in my hands.

Of course, since I didn't have any control over my body, it went off and starting spurting laser fire haphazardly around the room, causing everyone to run for cover. But it did break Leona's concentration and free me from her control.

I quickly stood up and backed away from the scene until I stood next to Jamie.

"What just happened?" I asked her.

She stared at me with wide eyes. "I wished you would have something to fight back with, and… then you did."

The truth dawned on me. "I guess we know what your gift is."

"Maybe you could clue me in, because I'm still a little fuzzy on that."

She looked terrified. I wondered what it was like not to grow up with radiation vaccines. I could hardly imagine a world where all my neighbors and friends didn't have carefully controlled supernatural abilities.

"This is a new one. I give you points for creativity." I smiled at her to help her adjust to the idea. "It's okay, Jamie. It's normal."

She glared at me. "Maybe it's normal in your wacked out Transient village full of freaks, but I'm not sure I want this *gift*."

"You're the one that jabbed yourself," I reminded her.

"After a night of feeling horrible and now an uncontrollable urge to provide people with weapons out of thin air, I'm definitely regretting that spur of the moment decision."

"My mother never liked having a gift, either. But when you fight it, you don't learn to control it or experience the benefits from it. You have to explore it and tame it like you would a wild animal. It takes time and practice. And patience."

I realized that Jamie wasn't the only one listening to me. Three other pairs of eyes were focused intently on my face.

"So," Leona said with a dark smile under narrowed eyes. "I can get better at this?"

I scrambled for words, but had none. I'd just given the future dictator of New York City the secret to her evil success.

Leona packed a bag, savagely throwing things inside. She roared at Arabella and Eli the entire time, citing all the betrayals and wrongs against her, and promised swift and costly payback. When she left, we all stared awkwardly at one another in silence.

"She's not usually that... outspoken." Arabella seemed to think she needed to apologize for her partner.

I gave her the same tolerant, but somewhat sarcastic expression I gave her older self every time she defended Leona.

"I'll have to take your word on that."

Eli took a step between Arabella and me, probably because of the laser rifle I was still holding across my chest, and put his hands on his hips. "Who are you and what are you doing in here?"

"Eli," Arabella patted his chest with her hand. "This is our grandson, Morris."

Eli didn't take quickly to the idea. In fact, he reached into a drawer and pulled out a gun. He didn't point it at me, but he displayed it clearly. "What are you talking about, Bella?"

Arabella cleared her throat and didn't meet his eyes. I'd never seen my wise grandmother so unsure before. "I solved it. There's a wormhole in the cap. We can travel in time."

His eyes found hers, wide and disbelieving. "Leona's formula?"

My young grandmother glanced at me uneasily. "Our grandson brought it to me. He said it was important I solve it before her. Important to the future."

The room got very quiet. Even Jamie stared at me somewhat reproachfully, as if I was responsible for the awkwardness.

"Don't look at me. I'm just on a mission from her," I said, pointing at Arabella. "Her elder version. From 2094."

"And she sent you here to do what?" Eli set the gun down and stood next to Arabella in what seemed like a protective position. I felt the affection hovering around them, drawing them together like magnets. It reminded me of my parents. I could see Roxy in her eyes, in his stubborn chin. I was awestruck at the chemistry of family, how two produced something altogether like them and altogether different at the same time.

"To give her the formula so we'll have a chance at defeating the kingdom Leona sets up for herself."

Eli glanced sideways at Arabella. "Kingdom?"

"I had a feeling she was on a dangerous path," Arabella said sadly. "I only hoped I was wrong."

Eli sighed as if he was giving up his ability to be skeptical about me and what I was saying. He held out his hand. "Good to meet you, grandson from the future."

It surprised me how quickly he accepted it then. I stared into the strong face of the man who had fathered my mother. My hand reached for his. I was struck with a sudden desire that my grandfather be proud of the man I was trying to become.

"I have questions," he said, looking from Arabella to me. "But I'm not going to ask them right now. Because we have a lot of work to do here. I'm sure you do as well."

I nodded. "Just one more thing. I have to secure the portal and find out what power source it's feeding on."

Arabella went to the transparent board, gesturing. "It's just theorems right now. We don't have much of a working prototype yet. As you can see, we have the bones, and they have been activated, but it will take some time to develop."

"We don't have a power source," Eli explained.

I shrugged. "You don't have a power source you *know* about."

"You're saying you know their power source?" Jamie asked, her arms folded across her chest.

"Not me. But she does. At least she does fifty years from now."

Eleven

If Jamie hadn't thought I was completely nuts already, she probably decided I was when she watched me trying to dig up the concrete foundation of the portal.

It took me half the day to even find the right place. Arabella made sure we had access, but that didn't mean we knew exactly where to go. My grandmother's journal hadn't been specific. She'd just said the portal site was buried in an underground bunker below the library. When Arabella left us at the old stairs that led to the basement, I realized there was a twenty foot tall maze of storage area that went on for both the length of the library and the length of the park behind it. I had to study the clues in the journal and walk back and forth across the complex a few times before I figured out the right spot. At least the space was empty. No one seemed to remember it was even there. But the floor was another few feet of solid concrete. I had to drill through it with the handy laser driller Jamie dreamed up out of thin air for me.

"You couldn't have come up with something that worked a little faster?" I asked after several buckets worth of sweat and another few hours of mind-numbingly boring work.

"Sorry," she said scornfully. "I'm not really taking requests for my gift at this point."

"I'll help."

We both looked up to see Eli standing over us. I started to argue, but he wasn't in the mood.

"Look, I'm going to help you, so just let it go. Arabella is on the lookout for Leona, so let's hurry up and get this done. Leona loves it down here, she'd be crazy angry if she found you here."

Several more feet of dirt underneath the concrete had to be dug out before we reached the metal shaft of the elevator that would take us to the power source protected deep within the earth. When we got in the elevator, we were lowered the rest of the way to the bottom with cables that squawked at us as if they were reminding us they were going on four hundred years old. Eli stayed above, looking out for Leona.

"Are you sure this is safe?" Jamie sniffed as she glared at the walls of our dangerous prison.

"No," I answered with plenty of sarcasm. "What made you think I was suggesting any of this was safe?"

"You're lucky I don't care about safety."

We finally reached the bottom and I felt the heaviness of so many layers of earth on top of us. Even though there was ventilation in the shaft and no reason to suspect we were in immediate danger of running out, my chest felt tight and I imagined it was hard to draw each breath.

"If I die down here, I'm going to kill you," Jamie promised.

"Good luck."

We found a cabinet that was futuristic in tech and design. I could easily see it was Transient-made. It was surreal to see the decay of the workings surrounding the power source, newer than me, yet centuries old, lost in the past.

"You built this?" Jamie fingered the age-old console from the future, covered with dust and vegetation.

"I will build it someday. I suppose I should be taking notes," I said.

She made a face. "That's cheating."

I pulled on the cabinet door, but it didn't move. I shook it hard and then yelled in frustration. Jamie made a scoffing sound as a laser rifle materialized in her hand. She shot at the lock mechanism and the doors fell open.

"Always doing things the hard way," she mocked. I grinned and climbed inside the cabinet.

"Is it wrong to be amazed by my own genius?" I called back to her. I surveyed the intricate network of wires and programs running into a square, transparent enclosure, similar to the prism we'd seen in 2033. It hovered in the air. It seemed to be providing a sort of electromagnetic pulse that leached into the air around it. My body trembled like it was possessed by a thousand minds.

"Your genius makes me feel weird," she said, eyeing the corners of the small chamber in distrust. "I think we should hurry up and get out of here."

"Just a second." One of the cables seemed to be detached. The prism must only be working at half power. I reached for the largest cable, thicker than my thigh, and tried to pick it up. It didn't budge. Vegetation had grown up over the sides of it and made it thicker, stronger and virtually impossible to lift the cord.

"Apparently I didn't know I'd need to plug it back in." I sighed, frustrated.

"Or you did it on purpose." Jamie shrugged.

I stared at her for a long moment as I tried to figure out what to do. "I need to go back to the beginning."

"The beginning of what? Time?" She said in a snarky voice. I stood up and climbed back out of the cabinet, walking toward her until she backed up against the wall. I smiled – maybe it was more of a sneer – and leaned into her face.

"The beginning of the portal. 1680."

I said the words, but I was more interested in how nice it felt to be standing so close to her. She glared at me with an interesting sort of challenge in her gaze that I didn't quite know how to interpret.

"You're using your power on me." The accusation came softly, in a voice I wouldn't have expected her to use if I was trying to manipulate her. Which I really hadn't been doing on purpose.

"Sorry." I didn't move away. I didn't want to feel the loss.

"If we stand this close together, it's going to be because I want it, not because you force me." Jamie's voice seethed, even as her fingers brushed against mine. I grabbed them without meaning to, reveling in her soft skin that disagreed with her hard demeanor.

"Do you want me to move?" I asked, waiting where I was. I wasn't sure what else to do.

The confrontational moment went on for a long time. Silence, except for the longsuffering hum of a four-hundred-year-old portal power source, filled the space.

"What I want," she said with great effort as her hands went to my chest and pushed me back. She went back to the power source. "Is to get this annoying little box fixed so we can go home."

We stood at opposite ends of the small room. I imagined I could see our tension mingling in the portal pressure. It had streaks of purple and short bursts of red as it lingered around Jamie.

"So what are we waiting for?" I held up my watch. "Let's go to 1680."

As I reached for the button that would hurl us to the far reaches of the past, the look on her face stopped me.

"What is it?" I took in her eyes, suddenly wide with uncertainty.

"That's my time, Morris. You said it yourself. I was there."

I stared at her, trying to understand what she wanted me to know. Maybe she just wanted me to recognize that this was a big deal.

"I get it, Jamie."

My soft response seemed to make her more relaxed.

"Let's get back to the surface," I said, motioning her to follow me back up. "I don't want to come through in 1680 this far below

72

ground without knowing how we get back out."

She mumbled something about a filthy Transient coward who forgot he could travel anywhere he wanted in time and space, but she followed me. When we were back on the street in daylight, I pulled her into a grove of trees where no one would see us jump out of time. I was about to give the command to the manipulator when a hand on my shoulder stopped me.

"I'm going with you."

I turned around to see my grandfather, Eli, standing beside me. I'd forgotten about him when he wasn't waiting at the opening of the tunnel.

"Where do you think we are going?" I asked him.

"I know you can travel in time. You're my grandson from the future, remember?"

I nodded slowly. "Why do you want to come with us?"

Eli stared me down. "I can guess what happens next in my story."

I didn't know what to say in response. I stammered, searching for the right words to set him at ease, yet knowing full well he would die.

He shrugged. "You are going to the past to fix the power source. Since I'm the one that's been working on that, I think I can help you."

I knew from his emotions that wasn't the whole story. "What's the real reason you want to go?"

He stared at me hard. His jaw was like steel, grinding as he tried to reign in the devastated feelings that surrounded him. "Look, I know I die. It's written all over your face. And my child will have to live without a father. I think I have a right to see her."

I didn't ask how he knew his child was a girl. I assumed Arabella had told him. I shook my head, sad that I had to tell him I didn't know where Roxy was. "I'm sorry, Eli. I have no idea where Roxy and Levi are. They are hiding somewhere in time to keep us all safe from Joe."

"Roxy." He said the name as if he were testing how it felt on his tongue. He considered me. I had the suspicion he knew something I didn't. Had he found the journal? I hadn't read the whole thing. Just the parts that I needed to know for the mission. It wasn't the Transient way to snoop.

"Listen, Eli. I'll make you a promise. If I find Roxy, I will bring her to you. Stay here and help Arabella. She's going to need you."

He looked at me for a long time. Finally, without a word, he stepped back and gave me a quick nod.

After the jolt of time and space, we touched down in a different world. Instead of high tech power and the hum of civilization, we landed in total darkness. We sat on the ground, waiting for our eyes to adjust and our brains to make sense of the surroundings.

"Why are we in the middle of nowhere?" Jamie whispered as if the sound of our voices would wake the devil.

"We're in the same place we were in 2050. But in 1680, it is wilderness. We'll have to walk south to find settled land."

Jamie seemed to take this information in stride. "Feels like home, doesn't it?" She stood up and turned in a circle, looking up at the stars that shined more brightly than I'd ever seen them. "Except our world is more worn out. Not as clear. The energy of the atmosphere is different."

I hadn't noticed until she said it, but she was right. "I never thought about the fact that the world is wearing out. But I think it's true. Makes you wonder what we could have done differently to make it stay the way it used to be."

"Maybe nothing. Maybe it's meant to be that way. But maybe it's because people got lazy and greedy." Her face was thoughtful in the faint glow from my timeband. "We used more than our share of resources. We stole what wasn't ours to take. We took it from our future."

It was a sober thought. I hoped she was wrong.

Jamie wasn't done with the conversation. "You know, say what you want about the SkyJacks, but besides the whole plundering and murdering issues, we don't take more than we need. We live simply."

"Joe steals people out of the past." I nudged her with my elbow as I stood up beside her and stared up at the sky. "He stole you."

"I didn't say he didn't." She was quiet after that. Words didn't seem necessary in the expanse we now saw.

Her voice sounded quiet and loud at the same time as she suddenly spoke into the quiet. "I expected I would feel something—being here where I came from. I thought it would feel like home."

"It doesn't?" I saw her hand fidgeting with the durable fabric of the Transient suit she was wearing. I reached for her. I held her fingers firmly, not letting her pull them away. Soon she relaxed and her fingers held mine in return. I swiped my thumb along the edge of hers and squeezed, still waiting for her answer.

"No. It feels cold and strange. I guess I don't belong anywhere."

"Everyone belongs somewhere," I disagreed.

She turned to me. "Then tell me where I belong, Morris."

You belong with me.

Something kept me from saying it. Maybe because I thought she wouldn't believe me, or she'd think I was manipulating her. Or maybe I didn't want to hear she didn't feel the same way.

We stood in silence for a time before I gently pulled on her hand. "I'm going to start digging. Why don't you get some sleep?"

Jamie didn't answer, but she sat down next to a smooth black rock and leaned back, staring at the stars as she folded her hands over her chest. I wanted to stay there and watch her, but I had to find a way down to that portal cabin. I supposed the only thing to do was kneel down in the dirt where we'd landed and start tearing up the earth.

It wasn't the most well-thought-out plan, I admit. But I didn't have much of an alternative available to me at the moment.

Suddenly, a compact laser digger appeared next to me. I looked back at Jamie and saw the smile on her face, though she didn't open her eyes.

"Thanks," I said with a grin and got to work.

An hour later, I hadn't made much headway when I felt the cool steel of a blade next to my ear.

"What in the worlds do you think you're doing?"

Twelve

I quickly rotated and put my hands in the air. I couldn't see much in the dim light, except that he was man holding a sword.

"I'm... digging," I said, not sure why he would care that I was digging in uninhabited territory. My clothes and my laser digger might scare him, but surely he couldn't see them well in the soft candlelight of the lantern he carried in the other hand.

Suddenly he grinned. "Hey, son."

It took me a good ten seconds to figure out why he was suddenly smiling and calling me his son. Because I *was* his son.

"Dad!"

I had one of those moments where I felt like a kid again, and I jumped up to hug him. He laughed and clapped me on the back in a manly way, pushing me back to get a better look at me.

"Morris, you're a man! When did that happen?"

I smiled. "I had no idea you were here! It's good to see you, Dad."

"What are *you* doing here?" Levi stood back and shook his head. "You're the last person I expected to see out here tonight."

"That's kind of a long story," I said. He grabbed my shoulder and nodded his head in the direction of what I assumed was New York Village.

"Come on home. Your mother is going to freak out."

I laughed. A man in seventeenth century breeches with a sword and a beard harboring more dirt in it than I had in my fingernails from digging, and he was using the term *freak out.*

I was enjoying the sight of him so much I almost left Jamie sleeping in the wilderness by herself.

"Wait!" I stopped him and ran back to the last place I'd seen her, sleeping on the rock. I shook her kind of hard. I guess I woke her up too quickly because she jumped up and had her arm around my throat before I could take a deep breath.

I waited for her to realize it was me and let me go. I didn't want to have to force her arm off my neck, but I couldn't breathe. Finally, she let me go.

"Sorry. You caught me off guard." She wiped the dirt on her clothes. She didn't seem that sorry.

My lungs screamed for air. I tried to play it cool while the oxygen returned to my body. When I could see clearly again, I saw that my father was smirking at me.

"So you've found a substitute for your mother."

I sighed and got to my feet, still fighting for my breath. "Something like that. Dad, this is Jamie Salvatore. Jamie—my dad."

"You happened to run into your dad in the year 1680?" She stared at me hard, like she was suspicious of the story.

I shrugged. "I don't know what to tell you. This is my family, in a nutshell."

She shrugged and gave Levi a short nod, though her hands didn't leave the laser rifle that had suddenly appeared in her hands.

He didn't seem surprised. I figured years of living with Roxy had conditioned him well. He motioned for us to follow him. "Let's go. I'm sure you both are hungry and tired. We'll find you some less conspicuous clothes before daylight as well. You are staying a while, aren't you?"

He stopped and turned to look at me. I nodded. "We'll stay a while."

I reached for Jamie's hand to help her up and didn't let go when she was standing. When I moved to follow my father, she hesitated.

"It's okay." I tugged on her hand. "You can trust them as much as me."

"Who said I trusted you?" She sniffed, but I felt her relax. I guess she believed me, because she started walking after me.

It didn't take us long to walk back to the village. It was mostly quiet, only disturbed by occasional raucous laughter from the tavern on the corner of Broadway. Levi led us silently down the path until we came upon a quaint little log cabin that looked well-kept, if not painfully simple.

"Help yourself to some bread and cheese on the table. There is well water in the bucket as well. I'll go wake Roxy."

I grabbed his arm to stop him. "Don't wake her up. I'm sure sleep is valuable in a place like this."

He looked undecided for a moment, but Levi finally nodded and went to light candles from the fire banked in the fireplace. "She's going to kill me for letting her sleep, you know."

I smiled. "I know."

Jamie watched us curiously as she tore bits of bread from her piece and ate. I watched her, thinking how pretty she looked in the soft yellow light from the tallow candles. "What are you thinking about?" I asked her.

"I don't know. Maybe wondering why your dad looks about five years older than you."

"Seven," I corrected.

"Oh, seven? That makes so much more sense," she said sarcastically.

"Hey, this becomes the standard when you come from a family of time travelers."

Levi smiled as he listened to our banter. He poured milk into rough wooden cups for both of us. "Gets even weirder, son. Just wait till you figure out who raised Roxy in her parents' place."

I eyed him. "Me?"

He raised an eyebrow. "You didn't hear that from me."

I didn't even try to process it. "Nothing surprises me."

Levi sat beside me and put his palm on my shoulder, squeezing with fatherly affection. It didn't seem strange to me. He was a good dad no matter what age he was.

The thought occurred to me. "Who was *your* father? Did you even know?"

Levi gave me a sad smile. "Nope. Leona took that secret to her grave."

"Leona's dead?"

A look passed over his face, was it regret? It didn't last long. He relaxed his features and even tried to suppress his emotions so I wouldn't see those, either. "Everything that happened... happened. No reason to revisit it. I always tell myself that my father was so busy saving the world, he couldn't be a dad to me. After all, that's what I expected you to believe."

"Not exactly," I argued. His frown went so deep I didn't know what else to say. He sighed as if he was still wrestling over that decision, though it had been made nearly two decades earlier. At least for me.

He looked up at me, working to temper his emotions again. Levi didn't want people seeing that he didn't have it all figured out. Well, he didn't want his son knowing, anyway. His voice was friendly and easy when he spoke. "I don't even know... how long has it been since you've seen us?"

"Quite a few years. Too many," I acknowledged, feeling a sudden lump in my throat.

"How old are you now? Seventeen?"

"Eighteen. Almost nineteen, actually."

"You're a man," he said again. He breathed the words softly, and I didn't think I'd really believed myself to be an adult until I'd heard him say the words. I nodded, sitting up taller in my chair.

"I'm a man. Just like you."

"And if you're here, you must have come up with the time manipulator. On your own."

I couldn't help my grin. "I did."

He nodded, and the proud sheen that appeared in his eyes for a moment betrayed his youth, making him seem much older. "Good. Have you gotten on okay without us?"

I was going to tell him of course I had, that I understood why we had to be apart and that I knew they'd been protecting me by hiding me in the future with my grandmother. But suddenly, the lump in my throat got so big I couldn't speak.

"I'm sorry." He shook his head. "We should have been together."

It helped, having him acknowledge it. I wanted to tell him how I'd missed them. Every day. But I couldn't get the words out.

"We think about you every day," he said quietly. "Roxy wonders what you're doing as she does her chores. She prays for you in church every Sunday. Even when the bay freezes over and the snow is a foot tall, she goes to church so she can pray for her boy. We haven't forgotten you, Morris. Not at all."

I nodded, imagining my determined mother braving the elements to do what she could for a son who wasn't even present in her world. It meant more than I could express. "I appreciate that, Dad," I managed. "I haven't forgotten you, either."

It was quiet for a long moment as I tried to shake of the emotions. Jamie had gone quiet as she listened to our conversation. I could see the melancholy haze around her person. How must she feel, not even knowing who her parents were?

"So, Jamie Salvatore, tell me about yourself," Levi asked, since I hadn't offered to explain who Jamie was and why she was there with me, hundreds of years in the past.

"I can't." She shrugged, not looking him in the eye. "I have no idea who I am. Jamie Salvatore isn't even my name."

Levi glanced at me, and I felt obliged to answer. "She was

stolen by Joe to become a SkyDweller. Stolen from this time."

Levi was surprised. "When?"

I shook my head as I took a gulp of sweet, creamy milk. "This year. In just a few months, actually."

"Did you try –" he began to ask, but I interrupted.

"I tried. And failed."

Levi's brows knit together in concentration. "There were a few children who disappeared nearly twenty years ago. We've only lived here for a few years, but people still talk about it. Some of the parents who lost children have a tradition of placing flowers on unmarked graves that were set up in the church cemetery to remember the children who were lost."

Jamie made a soft sound of frustration. "Joe's a leech. Sucking the life out of history."

Levi watched us thoughtfully. "At least the two of you were able to meet. Sometimes bad things lead us to good things."

Jamie met my eyes. "I haven't decided if that was a good thing yet."

A sudden sound in the doorway made us all look up. Roxy was standing there in her long white nightgown, a thick braid tossed over her shoulder, her eyes lit with fire and her fingers balled up in white fists at her sides. I had no idea why she was angry, but I was too glad to see her to worry about it. I stood up and heard the breathless wonder in my voice when I spoke.

"Mom."

She suddenly ran toward me. For a moment I was afraid she was going to hit me, but she jumped into my arms and wrapped her fierce embrace around my neck, which was probably just about the same amount of painful.

"What are you doing here? Why didn't you wake me up? Morris!"

She hit me a couple times on the shoulder and then resumed her painful hug.

When she finally let me go, she punched Levi's arm, I

assumed for not waking her up. Then she came back. She reached up to take my face between her hands, kissing me soundly on the cheek several times.

"You're taller than me! I can't believe I missed your growth spurt!"

"How do you even keep track? We've seen him so out of order." Levi chuckled.

Roxy turned to Jamie, whose presence she seemed to accept though she couldn't have had a single clue why she was there. "He was born three years ago. My son, taller than me, and he was born three years ago"

Jamie exchanged a glance with me. "He told me his family was weird."

"You have no idea." Roxy sat Morris down and opened the rickety cupboard above the table. "I'll make some hoe cakes and maple syrup. You must be starving."

"The bread and cheese are fine, Mom," I insisted, reaching around her to close the cabinet door. "Just sit down and tell me how you are."

"Do you think life here is really that interesting?" She looked at me as if I was crazy. "I get up every morning at the blasted crack of dawn and milk the ornery goat. Then I make food, sweep up bucket loads of dirt and grime, and take care of children all day. Never a thanks to be had from anyone, mind you. See? Not interesting. How about you tell us why you're here and why you brought Jamie?"

Roxy said her name as if Jamie were familiar to her. "Do you know her?" I didn't know how it could be, but both of them had easily accepted her presence, as if it weren't the first time they'd met her.

Roxy and Levi exchanged a glance that made me feel like they were keeping something major from me.

"Keep in mind, son, the last time we saw you, you were around forty. A lot is going to happen during your life." Levi left it at that, shaking his head like he wasn't about to say another word.

I grabbed Jamie's hand under the table before I really considered I was doing it. She didn't pull away from me. I looked at her and suddenly realized how proud I was to be able to introduce her to my parents. Even if they'd already met her in the future, which actually gave me an exciting sort of hope. "Joe stole Jamie from this time. Or he will soon."

This seemed to surprise Roxy. So she didn't know everything about Jamie.

"Joe?" Roxy seethed.

Jamie nodded. "I'm a sky dweller."

"Do we know what those are?" Roxy frowned at Levi. He shrugged, leaning back in his chair.

"Joe's army," Jamie explained. "I've spent the past ten years trying to annihilate your son's village."

"Oh," Roxy said, as if Jamie had just told her she'd spent the last ten years knitting an afghan. She popped a piece of bread in her mouth. "This is good. I make good bread now, Morris."

I nodded. "I noticed."

"At least my life will count for something," she quipped. "So are you two...together?"

Levi elbowed her and she shot him an unappreciative look. "I'm the *mother*. I can ask."

I glanced at Jamie uncertainly. Were we? I wasn't sure how to quantify our relationship, but Roxy wouldn't be satisfied until I gave her an answer. Jamie only stared at me with some kind of challenge in her eyes. I had no idea what it meant.

"Not as together as you two were in the blizzard." I raised an eyebrow, looking back at my dad.

Roxy narrowed her eyes at me and shot a look at Levi. "Why does everyone in our future know about the storm like they were there?"

Levi made a face. "If I'd known the whole collective of my

descendants were watching, I may have given a little more thought to the whole thing."

"No, you wouldn't have." Roxy waved him off, her eyes focused on me. "Is this relationship headed in that direction?"

I felt Jamie's inquisitive eyes on me again. I shrugged, embarrassed. "I don't know, Mom. There are other concerns."

She nodded, probably satisfied that I wasn't on the verge of anything she needed to attempt to control. "So why are you here?" she asked.

"I came to adjust the original portal support unit. I tried to fix it in 2050 when Arabella created time travel and there was too much overgrowth."

"We'll have to put some sort of protective barrier around it. I should have thought of that before," Levi mused.

"You saw my mother?" Roxy asked.

I nodded. "And Leona. She was being Leona, of course."

I didn't miss the sad expression that passed over Levi's face. It made me wonder again about the history they shared. I'd been told what my grandmother believed I needed to know, but Arabella wasn't about revealing more than she must. I was beginning to disagree with her methods. If we were supposed to correct the past, shouldn't I know what I was up against? Shouldn't I have the whole picture so I knew how it was supposed to go?

Roxy gave Levi a knowing glance. "So it has begun." It was quiet for some time after that.

Thirteen

It was weird, but I identified with 1680 a lot more than I had 2050. Especially after my father gave me his spare breeches and tunic so I'd blend in.

You'd think four hundred years in the past would be a different world, but people were still people, and the simple, structured life was something I was familiar with. The complete absence of tech was different. Almost freeing. Here I was under no obligations to save everybody and make the world right again. People just lived to survive here. No one felt compelled to save generations from certain destruction. Except in church, which Roxy insisted Jamie and I attend with her.

"Reverend Hegemen," she whispered to me as we sat in their pew. The man banged on the podium and shouted angrily at the people in a Dutch accent. "Sophie and I lived with him and his wife when we first came here."

I almost asked who Sophie was, but I had the feeling I wasn't prepared to know.

Roxy patted my knee. "Don't worry. The reverend just sounds angry because he cares."

Levi smiled at me over the top of her head, and I chuckled. Until I saw the look on Jamie's face. She was watching the pastor closely.

My father?

I heard the words clearly from her mind. But she wouldn't look at me.

Could it be?

When the service was over, we stepped out of the small church building. Reverend Hegemen was standing near the door talking with a group of men. I was surprised to see a smile on his face.

"I told you he wasn't as bad as he sounded," Roxy said with a nudge. "Don't be so judgy, Morris."

I laughed. "Stop reading my mind, Mom. That's against the law where I come from."

"It's not here." She shrugged and went over to the group of men.

"Come meet my..." Roxy stopped herself in time. "My brother."

Reverend Hegemen stepped away from the group and came to us. He shook my hand with a warm expression.

"This is Morris. And his friend J–"

"Anika," Jamie said suddenly, almost whispering the name. "My name is Anika."

"My daughter's name is Anika," he said. "She's just a little thing, but she has your coloring."

Jamie took a step back. Her eyes were wide and scared. She turned around and took off running.

I thought she would be headed back to Levi and Roxy's little dwelling, but as I jogged after her, I noticed she was headed toward the wall.

"Where are you going?" I called after her, but she ignored me. She lifted her skirts into her arms so she could run faster.

When she reached the wall, she stopped abruptly in front of a house.

"This is my home," she said breathlessly. "I lived here."

I came to stand beside her. "And your name is Anika? Are you the pastor's daughter?"

She suddenly looked at me and gave a manic laugh. "I'm a pastor's daughter, Morris."

"It wouldn't have been my first guess," I admitted with a grin.

She looked back at the house, her face somber again. "Margaret. Her name is Margaret."

"Your mother?"

She glanced at me and nodded as she looked back at the house.

I noticed movement at the side of the house and motioned for her to follow me. We went to the rickety fence where a woman was kneeling beside the garden, cutting some wildflowers from the edge of the yard.

"And here is a lovely yellow daffodil for my beauty," she said softly, hooking the stem of the flower into a little girl's hair curly blonde hair. The little girl beamed, and I was breathless at how pretty she was.

"Anika," I said, trying the sound of her name.

"She is Anika," Jamie said dully. "I am just Jamie now."

She wouldn't say anything else as she turned abruptly and walked home. But I heard her thoughts.

I had a mother. She loved me. How did I forget her?

"Sometimes I wish time travel had never been invented," I admitted to my father as we walked to the portal site, leaving Jamie and Roxy to do the chores and mind the children. It had been hours since church, but Jamie refused to talk about what I had heard from her mind.

"What makes you say that?" Levi didn't seem surprised by my admission, but curious.

"Being able to go to the past or the future makes you responsible for it, in a way." I kicked a large stone on the path and watched it skip into the woods and hit a tree.

"Do you resent being elected the family time traveling history fixer?" Levi asked with a smile.

"It would have been nice to be asked. Grandmother just assumes."

"Have you talked to her about it? She's never been the unreasonable type. That was *my* mother."

I nodded. "Leona is a piece of work. What was it like growing up with her?"

Levi shook his head with a mirthless laugh. "I was the son of a ruthless dictator who controlled every part of her subjects' lives at the same time she acted like she was their loving rescuer. She gave me everything she ever thought I should want, and never asked what I actually wanted. It was lonely."

"But then you met Roxy."

He smiled. "Then I met Roxy. And life has never been the same. I went from a woman who had no concept of love to a woman who loves so fiercely it's terrifying sometimes."

I laughed. "I haven't spent much time with her, but I do get that impression."

"You will." He nodded with certainty in his promise. "You'll have plenty of time to get to know her."

I watched him for a moment and then nodded. "I believe you."

"So now that you're here, and we're alone, and you're becoming a man, is there anything you want to talk about? I'm not the wise old dad I should be at this point in your life, but I'm a little further down the road than you. I might be able to help."

I didn't have any specific questions that had been burning in my psyche, but I did realize at that moment what it meant to me that he would ask. It was the nature of father-love. I'd missed it.

"I think I'm good, Dad. But I'm glad you asked."

He nodded. "Typical teenager," he teased.

The portal site was in view when a question occurred to me. "How did you know when you loved Roxy? I mean, *really* knew."

He eyed me curiously, but didn't comment on Jamie. "I knew the moment I laid eyes on her that I didn't ever want to be away from her. But she didn't know it for a long time. There were years of waiting involved."

I nodded slowly.

"It's okay to wait. To make sure something is right. Love can be complicated, and no matter what anyone tells you, you can't come back from it without being changed."

It felt weird being advised by my not-even-thirty-year-old father. Weird, but really good.

We spent the rest of the afternoon finding a solution to keep the portal source free of invading vegetation for four hundred years. It involved a couple quick trips to the future for supplies. The second time Levi asked me to go I remembered my promise to Eli.

"Do you think Roxy would come with me?"

Levi shrugged. "I think Roxy would love to get away for a few minutes."

I went home and found her scrubbing a floor while she grumbled about meaningless chores that were undone as fast as they were done. When I asked her to join me, she could barely contain her excitement. She cleaned up and I entered the 2050 date into my timeband.

I made sure to coordinate specifically to the portal room that time. When we came through, a young Arabella stood nearby.

"I'm not sure she's ready to meet you at this point," I said, taking Roxy's hand and pulling her out of the room before Arabella saw us. I walked quietly down the hall until I saw Eli. He was leaning over a metal cabinet full of wires.

"Is that my father?" Roxy's voice went vulnerable. She sounded so young. "But he died."

I squeezed her hand. "He didn't die. Not yet. And he asked to see you all grown up."

Since he never will. I didn't say it, but we both thought it at the same time.

She only let herself be afraid for another moment before she nodded resolutely. She stepped forward and cleared her throat. "Dad?"

I felt a lump in my throat when my grandfather turned around and saw my mother.

She fidgeted with her hands and gave him an awkward smile. "Hi."

He inhaled sharply. His tool fell to the floor and he stood there for a long minute.

"Oh, you look like your mother." He stared at her as tears filled his eyes. "Roxy, is it?"

She nodded.

"My little star," he said softly. He came to her and put his hand on her cheek. "It's so good to meet you."

"I'm sorry I'm so old," Roxy said, then made a face at her own words. Her face flushed and made her look anything but old.

"Don't be sorry." He smiled. "You've given me a gift that will give me the strength to get through what is going to happen. I can see with my eyes that you will be okay even though I won't."

Roxy glanced at me. *How much does he know?*

Only that he will die when you are very young.

She nodded and turned back to him. She reached for his hands and stared at them. "So many times, I've imagined this moment, and I thought of so many things I'd like to tell you. So many questions. But now that we are here, I can't think of any of them."

"I know what you mean," he said, his voice trembling slightly.

They stood quietly for another moment. Finally, he held her hands tightly and shook them a bit. "Just tell me that you found your place. Your purpose. That you didn't play it safe, but you went for your dreams."

She lifted shining eyes to him. "I tried to play it safe. But somehow, I never got away with it. The people who love me didn't let me get away with it. I've found everything I couldn't even imagine for myself. I found love, I found family, and I learned how to lead."

It was strange hearing Roxy's secret thoughts as she whispered them to a father she would never know. Roxy didn't usually open up that much. I hoped he knew what a treasure she was giving him.

"Then I can accept my fate." Eli nodded, sighing, as if in relief. He looked at me. "Thank you."

Levi and I spent a couple more days on the portal source. Finally, we were confident it would be ready for the future. We headed back to the village, quiet.

When we got home it was nearly dark. I considered the town. This Manhattan was peaceful, at least compared to the other ways I'd seen it recently. As we headed up the lane toward the little house they lived in, a screech assaulted the night air.

"Roxy!" Levi started running. I followed him inside to find Roxy on the back of a man with her arms and legs wrapped tightly around his torso and neck. I recognized the clothing immediately.

Joe.

At the same time, I noticed Jamie standing next to them, her arms folded across her chest in a sort of disinterest.

Levi went for a locked chest at the foot of the bed behind the curtain, but by the time he'd found the key, unlocked it and produced a laser pistol, Roxy had managed to disorient Joe enough that he got too close to the fire and burned his bare arm. He yelled and threw Roxy off, but Levi managed to hit him with the laser rifle in the time it took him to switch his focus from her to him.

Just when I was thinking the situation was in hand, a SkyJack sword appeared in Joe's uninjured hand. He sliced Roxy's arm and managed to get his footing as he smirked at Jamie.

"I knew you'd come through for me, baby. Looks like you have a new talent, too. You got the vaccine?"

"I didn't get any extras," Jamie said uncertainly, as if she was afraid to displease him.

He took a step toward her and lifted his burned arm to put a hand on her cheek. "It's in you, though. We can figure out a way to make it ourselves. You did good."

I stared at Jamie in disbelief, hardly able to believe what I was seeing with my own eyes. "Jamie? What's going on?"

She looked at me, but I didn't see any regret or uncertainty about what she was doing. The only choice I had was to believe she'd betrayed me. Plain and simple.

Anger surged up and made my face feel like it was on fire. "You were playing games with me the whole time?"

She shrugged like she didn't have the energy to care about my feelings. "We all have our loyalties."

"After everything? You just walk back to him?"

She took a step closer to Joe.

Joe scoffed. "You didn't really think she'd turn away from family just for a kid with a time machine, did you? Didn't you see this was the plan all along?"

I was humiliated. My hand shook as I gripped the laser pistol. I couldn't believe I was thinking about using it on the girl I'd just told my dad I thought I loved.

Laser pistol. I looked down in my hand and saw the weapon I hadn't previously remembered having on my person.

I met her eyes. She stared at me with the same indifferent expression, but I thought I saw something behind it. Maybe she wasn't betraying me after all.

Suddenly Roxy's voice filled my mind. *It's Joe. His gift is the ability to make himself seem stronger than he really is. Like you have no hope of going against him. He's been able to trick me with it, so I can imagine someone he's been in control of since her childhood would have no ability to fight it. She may not be betraying you. Don't do anything you'll regret.*

At first, I thought Roxy was talking out loud, but a quick survey of the room told me I was the only one who'd heard the words. Well, maybe my dad heard. Levi was nodding.

"I suppose that time machine watch you're wearing is designed only to work with your DNA," Joe said, musing as if he had no concern whatsoever that he was in any danger of losing control of the situation.

"Of course. It's useless if you try to use it." I wasn't completely sure it was the truth, especially since I remembered Arabella saying something about Joe being Leona's son and therefore my uncle and blood relative. But it wouldn't hurt for him to be in doubt, I figured.

I took a couple steps closer. "Let her go."

He laughed. "I'm not making her do anything. I can't help it you got duped."

Roxy seethed. "We all know what you did to her, you lousy mudsill! You stole her from her parents and made her your killing machine. You're sick. Sicker than I ever gave you credit for. And you just keep coming back!"

Roxy's spiteful words only increased Joe's amused reaction. "Roxy, you hurt me. As if I'd ever kidnap little kids and force them to be my soldiers. Day after day, making them line up and kill Transient slime to break them in." He laughed and put an arm around Jamie's shoulders. "Jamie was a special project. She made her first kill when she was eight. Didn't even hesitate or whine like some of the other kids. She just pulled the trigger and dropped the enemy. I was always proud of her."

A flash crossed Jamie's face, but it disappeared as quickly as it was there. I could have imagined it. I needed a plan, and I needed to let her go. But I found I couldn't do it.

"I'm not leaving here without her, Joe. You lost this one," I bluffed.

Joe suddenly came at me, his face twisted with rage. "I didn't lose anything, Morris Koenig. You can't have her."

As if to completely humiliate me, Jamie took his side. "It's okay, Morris. We both knew that I couldn't really become someone like you. I'm too far gone. I've done too much. Maybe

I'll see you around. Maybe not."

She leaned up and kissed my cheek, and I thought it was weird how sweet and lovely she smelled. You wouldn't think she was a mindless slave of a murderer. I wanted nothing but to hold her, never mind everyone standing around gawking at us.

I grabbed her hands. "Jamie," I said, and my voice sounded way too vulnerable. Joe scoffed. Jamie's face remained passive as she pulled her hands back and turned away from me.

"I don't know how you think you're going to get away, Brant," I told Joe. "I have the timeband."

'Do you?" Joe shook his head, reaching to take something from Jamie's hand. "I'm pretty sure I have it."

I looked down and saw my bare wrist. Jamie had taken the timeband off as I was distracted. Maybe she even wished it off of me.

Joe backed up a couple steps as he snapped on the band. He was rough as he grabbed Jamie's arm and pulled her back with him.

"See you around," he said as he reached for the button.

I knew by the light searing into the small hut that it was going to work for him. I turned back, wanting one last look at my parents before I jumped into the time stream with them. Roxy was reaching toward me. Levi nodded to me, as if to say I had his support no matter where I went or what I had to do.

"Will I ever see you again?" I called to them as the light began to grab me away and everything turned to stars.

Roxy nodded and swallowed hard. "Our time is coming. See you there."

And then they were gone, fading away like images on a screen as reality shifted and perspective changed. When we were transferred back to our own Manhattan in the future, my face was wet with tears shed four hundred years before.

"Bye, Mom. Bye, Dad." I whispered before I turned around and prepared to fight Joe with every last ounce of Koenig and

LINEAGE

Eisen strength in me.

Fourteen

When I turned around, Joe and Jamie were gone. With my timeband.

I got my bearings and realized I was standing in my own yard. No wonder they'd ran so fast. I took a deep breath and headed into the house to tell my grandmother I'd lost the time manipulator controls. To Joe.

As I expected, she wasn't happy. But she wasn't surprised, either. She made me dinner and sent me to bed. I was thankful for familiar Transient food and my plain, solid bed, but I tossed and turned thinking about losing Jamie and the timeband. I needed a plan to get her – and get my time manipulator back.

When the sun finally rose and I got up to get dressed, I saw something sticking out of my pocket. I pulled out a weathered, faded piece of paper torn from an old book. I saw text in the corner, written in familiar handwriting.

1. May 10, 1854, Lying-In Asylum on Marion Street, New York City
2. November 11, 2057, New York County Courthouse.
3. October 5, 2058, New York Library and Research, portal room

4. December 25, 2059, Square in front of newly constructed Crystal Citadel
5. June 21, 2060, Border at the Lincoln Tunnel.
6. That same night, Lafayette Street across from Astor Library.
7. November 9, 2067, the same place
8. June 21, 2074, Portal room, Crystal Citadel
9. September 27, 2074, the same place
10. December 25, 1776, Abandoned shed just to the east of Trenton, NJ.
11. January 14, 1777, Central Park area
12. Transient Village, 2116

"What is it?"

I turned around to see Arabella standing in the doorway.

"Roxy." I looked back at the list. "I think she wants me to go to these places."

I handed her the ancient piece of paper and she studied it with a frown that I didn't understand. She handed it back to me. "Maybe it's time, then."

"Well, whether it is or not, I'm going to need to get the timeband back first, unless I make a new one."

"It would be better if you get it back, obviously," she said, turned and heading down the stairs. I followed her. Before I reached the bottom, the alarms were going off.

"SkyJacks!"

We both sprang into action, grabbing our protective gear and weapons that waited in their locked space beside the door. On the way out, she suddenly caught my arm and made me stop. She stared at me firmly.

"What are you going to do if you see Jamie?"

I tossed the laser rifle over my shoulder. "I'm going to get my timeband back."

The battle turned out to be the worst we had ever known. So many casualties were lined up on the side of the road an hour later I wondered if there would be any of us left. Joe seemed to get stronger and stronger while we kept getting weaker. We needed a new plan. We needed better, stronger weapons, capable of dealing with SkyJack brutality. Our people were too soft. I would change that when I was leader. If I had anyone left to lead, that is.

The last few SkyJacks taunted me as they ran to their ship and flew upward, easily missing my laser fire. The boat sailed the sky, defying gravity as the heavy frame creaked and tilted and soared on the thermals.

A whimpering caught my attention. Someone nearby was wounded.

I found her pretty quickly. It was a SkyJack woman, decked out in leather and lace and long, tattered ribbons. Her eyes were hidden behind thick black painted circles and her wrists were shackled with rough iron bracelets. Even as I approached, she groaned and held up her spear.

"Stay away," she growled.

I hadn't been sure until I heard her voice. Jamie.

I came closer and squatted beside her, assessing the damage. She'd been caught in the chest with a laser rifle blast. There was no way she would survive the wound.

"Why did you do this to yourself?" I couldn't help asking the question. This could have been avoided. It should have. "Following Joe is a death wish."

"I know."

Her words were sullen and she didn't offer any other explanation. I saw my timeband hidden under the heavy iron cuffs, so I took it off her arm, dusted it off and put it on my own wrist.

I stood up, undecided. I almost left her there. No one in the Transient village would care. In fact, they would ask questions if

I saved a SkyJack who had just attacked and killed our people. Maybe it was right to walk away. Maybe I was crazy for hesitating.

But I stopped. My feet wouldn't move any further away from her. I glanced backward and saw her struggling to lift her arm long enough to drag her body into the nearest bush. She would wait there to die like an animal.

I swallowed hard, squeezed my eyes shut. What should I do? Why did I feel so disgusted with myself for leaving her there? Why did I feel like I was losing someone important? Someone worth fighting for?

I turned and kneeled next to her. She'd given up her struggle to get out of the path. Her eyes were glassed over and blood dripped from her red lips. I only had seconds to decide.

I put my hand on her chest and summoned the healing energy I wasn't sure I possessed. I'd seen my father do it. Maybe I could, too. I watched in surprise as light glowed from my fingertips and reached to her skin, slowly restoring the smooth flesh and healthy complexion. In moments she was able to sit up and stare at my hands.

"What did you just do?"

I didn't want her to know I was just as surprised as she was. "I healed you. You're welcome." I stood up, prepared to leave her again. My feet felt as heavy as boulders and I almost blacked out from weakness, but I started walking. I steeled myself against her pleas for me to stop.

"Wait! Morris!"

I ignored her. She ran after me and grabbed my arm hard.

"You're acting like I betrayed you on purpose! I had no choice! You should know better than anyone that he owns me, Morris! I have to do what he says."

"You don't have to. You can choose differently, even if it's uncomfortable."

She hesitated. "I don't know how. Teach me."

"The same way you resist me." I shrugged and kept moving. She stayed in stride with me.

"Morris, I don't want to be a SkyJack. You have to believe me. Let me come with you."

I sighed and stared up at the sky beginning to display a variety of bright stars. They would witness any further lapse in judgment on my part.

"Jamie, you're killing me." I said. But I couldn't walk away.

"I never knew I wanted anything better until I met you." She almost pouted as she said the words. "This is your fault. You're probably controlling me as much as he is, but at least you have better standards."

I laughed harshly and shook my head. "Thanks, I think."

We stared at each other for a long moment. It was awkward, but it was also intense. It was crazy how much life was pouring out of a girl who'd been all but dead two minutes earlier. Her cheeks were rosy and her voice breathless, her eyes like stars as she stared up at me.

As I was feeling ashamed of myself for having the thought cross my mind that I'd like to kiss her, she suddenly jumped into my arms. Her mouth pressed hard against mine and in that moment, I was in the best place I'd ever been in my life.

I think that was the moment I decided I didn't care what she'd done, who she was or even what she could do to me or my people. I wanted her in my life, and I wasn't willing to go on without her. I'd do whatever it took to make it happen.

Little did I know that realization was about to get its first major test.

"Maybe I won't kill you since you saved what belongs to me."

I turned around to see Joe's signature smirk peering from narrowed eyes. He was there to take Jamie and kill me.

"Come on, Salvatore." He motioned for her to join him.

She gave me a wild look. "Don't trust me and don't worry about me. Just run."

101

I almost laughed; the thought was so ridiculous. As if I'd let her be his slave again. Over my dead body – that was the only way it would happen.

"We're not playing that game anymore, Jamie. I'm either in or I'm out. I decided I'm in," I said as I turned toward Joe.

Her expression only became more frantic when she saw I'd already decided what was going to happen in this scenario, and it didn't involve turning anything over to Joe and hightailing it back to the Transient village.

"Looks like the winner takes the girl." Joe shrugged, as if to say he was okay with that. "I was just giving you the chance to save yourself."

Joe lunged first. I shoved Jamie out of the way and threw myself at him before he could squeeze the trigger of his laser rifle. I pushed it hard and it flew off into the bushes. He grabbed for mine so I threw that one, too, determined to make it a weapon-free fight.

The next thing I tried was my gift. As I tried to maintain my position over him, I held his arms down and focused all my attention on calming him down.

"Just give it up, Brant," I said. "She's one girl. Is she really worth all this?"

He sneered at me. "You think you can control me? You're a child trying to play tricks, but I'm a master at it."

And looking into his expression, I could see the absence of fear or struggle. He was not afraid of me in the least. And the heavy feeling I had, like someone was sitting on my chest and cutting off the air in my lungs, told me he had already begun to have his effect on me.

"Morris, run," Jamie urged. "We'll find a way. You're just going to get yourself killed."

In one motion, Joe grabbed my neck. Without breaking his hold, he stood up while I sputtered and gasped for air. Blackness edged the corners of my vision.

It was then I noticed the sound of something big – something huge – crashing against the tops of the trees above us. I felt the whine and complaint of massive amounts of decking as it careened through the air right above our heads. Joe loosened his hold for a moment, and I looked up.

A sky ship loomed over us as if it had appeared out of thin air.

I looked at Jamie, staring intensely at the sky, and knew what had just happened, though it was hard to believe it.

"You did this?"

She didn't break her concentration long enough to nod. Her face was red with effort and her eyes narrowed in extreme focus. A rope swung low through the trees, connected to the mast of the immense ship, and it flung itself right toward me. I kicked Joe in the chest hard enough to make him fall back and reached for Jamie the same moment I reached for that rope. I held on with every bit of arm strength I possessed, and we rose up into the sky.

We shimmied up the rope and onto the deck. Jamie ran along the spar deck and up the stairs to the grand wheel turning haphazardly to the right and then to the left as the ship took whatever direction the wind instructed.

She put all her weight into stopping the motion of the wheel, but it wasn't until I came up and put my arms around her and grabbed it that we began to make some headway in controlling the massive ship.

After we got it flying in a straight path, the wind stopped whipping us around and the sea of the sky grew calm and inviting. Stars were starting to reveal themselves in the darkening blue of the evening sky. I felt Jamie relax under my arms and lean back against me, and neither of us moved for a long time.

"I think I love you," I whispered before I thought about what I was saying. I meant it, but I wasn't sure she was ready to hear it. She didn't say it back, but she turned around and let me take over the steering while she took over the kissing. It was hard to have a coherent thought for a few seconds. When I could think again, I steered the ship toward the open ocean.

I didn't even have to ask if she wanted to join me on my mother's errands to the past. When we came up for air, I leaned around her and set the coordinates for the first visit Roxy had instructed.

I was kissing her again when we vanished from the ship and sent it careening into the night sky full of stars. We entered the time stream and went to the past, riding the waves of exhilaration. Love was waking up for the first time within the wild, unexplored loops of history.

Fifteen

May 10, 1854
New York City, Marion Street

For a moment Jamie and I stood on the street together, smiling at each other. It took a few seconds to realize we were oddly dressed and about to be run over by a team of horses who didn't understand how we could just appear in front of them in the street. They reared back and their owner shouted at us, shaking his fist and standing in his seat for a moment until we got out of the way. We jumped off the cobblestone and onto the boardwalk.

"Where are we?" Jamie asked. She only sounded curious, not angry. I was relieved she didn't mind being there. I wasn't sure I wanted to do this trip on my own.

"We are in New York City in the spring of 1854. My mother told me to come here first. I'm not sure why."

"You can't think of anything that would have happened in 1854 that relates to you?"

I shrugged. "I can only imagine."

We were standing in front of a three-story Federalist style building labeled only by a small brass plaque on the door that read *No. 38 Marion Street.*

"What should we do?" Jamie eyed me curiously.

I stared at the door, wanting to knock, but knowing our clothes would cause a stir.

"We need something better to wear."

I led her into the alley next to the building and we walked until we found a line of clothes strung across a bottom floor set of windows from one building to the next. I quickly pulled off a set of trousers, shirt and coat for myself. Jamie followed my lead and quickly found a dress that might fit her. We stepped into the shadow and quickly pulled the clothes over our own. Jamie had to remove some of the gaudy layers of her intimidating SkyJack outfit and wipe the dark outline of kohl from her eyes. She tied her wild braided hair into a partially tamed bun. I smiled at her.

"You'd fool me," I said.

We stole back out of the alley before someone saw us. We approached the door of the building we'd faced as we came through the time stream.

"This is the Lying-in Asylum, according to Roxy," I explained as I knocked firmly on the door. "So be prepared to be my unfortunate sister."

"What?" She narrowed her eyes and huffed just as the door whisked open.

A woman with thin lips and white hair pulled into a tight bun gazed at us severely. "Well? State your business."

I cleared my throat. "Hello, madam. I am looking for an arrangement for my sister. Her husband was killed and she is expecting –"

Apparently, that was what the woman needed to hear. She motioned us inside.

We waited in the office for some time, but after filling out some paperwork, another woman came to show Jamie to her room.

"What now?" Jamie asked as we followed her up the stairs.

"We find whoever we're supposed to find here. I'm sure Roxy

wants me to see something that happens here tonight," I whispered as I glanced through the small window of every door we passed.

It didn't take long to figure it out. All I had to do was hear the screaming – and cursing – coming from one of the rooms to the right.

"So sorry," the woman said in embarrassment. "Usually, they take the laboring mothers to the hospital wing in the back to give birth. This mother must have progressed too quickly."

Jamie was shown to a room several doors down. The woman gave her instructions and then looked at me. "I'll see you out, sir."

"Give me a moment?" I gave her my best smile. I made sure my gift was at full power, even laying my hand on her shoulder as I charmed her socks off. "I'd just like to say goodbye. I'll meet you downstairs in a minute."

"Oh, brother," Jamie said, rolling her eyes. "You're shameless."

The woman, of course, couldn't resist me. "That's not how we usually do things, but I won't tell if you won't." She chuckled as she left the room.

I gave Jamie a smug smile.

"Ridiculous," she said.

"You love ridiculous."

"So do you know why you're here now?" She folded her hands across her chest.

"I do. This is where my father was born."

She raised an eyebrow. "Your father was born a hundred and twenty-some years before you?"

"Technically, I was born in 1776. So, I was born nearly a hundred years before my father."

She laughed at that. "Your family is bizarre. You know that, right?"

"I've come to terms with it."

We went back into the hallway and crept back to where the woman had been giving birth. Things had gone quiet, so I figured it was over.

The door was open a crack so I gave it a push. We both looked in the room to see a young Leona with red-blonde hair cascading down the back of her frilly white nightgown. She peered from lovely eyes and a flawless complexion at a squirming bit of redness wrapped up in her arms.

"You are a beautiful boy," she whispered, more vulnerable than I ever imagined I'd see my infamous grandmother, Leona. "You'll be better than your brother. You'll be as brave and striking as your father. You are my strong, handsome Levi."

"That's your father?" Jamie whispered. I nodded in speechless awe.

Leona had no idea we were watching her. She was spellbound by her new son, who watched her curiously with large, alert eyes. She continued. "You are born in the perfect time. Here they are reasonable. They function by rules and expect citizens to follow. They build grand architecture and give careful thought to every decision they make."

She looked out the window. "I could build a world like that, Levi. A world for you. I could lead the people of our time to respect rules and order and beauty again. I will. And I will give you my legacy, my son. You will be the greatest ruler that ever lived."

I suddenly felt sad. I turned around and started walking back downstairs. Jamie followed me and tucked her hand into mine.

"You know he'll become a good man." Her reminder was quiet, as if she was afraid it was the wrong thing to say.

I nodded. "But she'll never get it. She'll always think she's the answer and she's going to hurt so many people because of that belief."

Jamie didn't speak. I stopped and looked into her eyes. "What if I made sure she never accomplished her plans? I could do that tonight."

"Morris –"

"It's my duty," I rushed on. "I've been told that my entire life."

Jamie searched my expression. "I understand the temptation. And you're not shocking me. I'm a SkyJack. I've done far worse. But would it solve anything? You can't be sure of that. The only thing you can be sure of is that it will change *you*."

Her words made the turmoil boiling in my chest settle. I could see clearly again. She was right.

"Let's go. Roxy's list isn't getting any shorter." She fingered the paper that peeked out from behind my timeband.

We took off the clothes we'd stolen and put over our own clothes, and folded them neatly in a pile at the top of the stairs. I entered the next information, and the room began to swirl and distort as time carried us away, leaving a mother to bond with her son and begin to imagine the kingdom she would create on his behalf. At the expense of everyone else.

Sixteen

November 11, 2057
New York County Courthouse

We stood in front of an old building. For nearly a century and a half, the County Courthouse had stood firm in its position on Centre Avenue. It had stayed rooted in place through the blackout and the war, and here it stood, a testament to its builders as well as to the determination of those who had protected the iconic image through all the fiery trials New York had experienced within those long years.

Jamie started up the stairs, of which there were many. I surveyed the crowd of New Yorkers, plain and white in their dress and neat in their appearance. They had been a people who had learned the hard way that it was better to fit in. To be pleasant. No one wanted to draw attention to themselves as in the very old days of free America and even freer New York City.

"2057," Jamie mused as we opened the large doors. A smart sign displayed the date and news in holograms above the rotunda. "It's weird. There's tech, but not really in the hands of the people."

"The blackout made tech completely unusable for months, even years in some places. When the electricity finally came back

110

on in the bigger cities, the disparity between rich and poor had become striking. Only the elite could afford technology. Government flaunted its use, but most people still lived in refugee camps, barely surviving."

"Where are we headed?"

I stared at the large hologram of a friendly-faced, yet plastic-looking woman, explaining all the rules of the courthouse and directing people in the ways they should go. Something she said caught my attention.

"Leona Koenig versus the state of New York, Courtroom A at the top of the staircase."

"I guess that's why we're here." I sighed and took her hand as we made our way up the stairs.

I had to use my timeband to get us through the doors, as they were heavily guarded by security carrying the first prototypes of laser rifles. I was getting pretty good at using time travel tech to move around and stay unnoticed at the same time. We sat in the back of the dark courtroom. It was simple in design compared to the ornate rotunda with the glass dome and intricate paintings. Gas lights spurted and crackled as they worked to give light to the room, though computer generated images hovered above the seats. I found Leona, sitting in the position of defendant at the long table in the front. She sat regally, her head held high and a smile pulling at her lips as she met the eyes of the men and women in the jury seats. I could feel their intimidation as they quickly looked away. Leona glanced over at Eli and Arabella and an icy glare passed over her expression before she looked away and veiled her disgust.

"Eli Eisen, please approach the bench."

My eyes searched the room hungrily until they could feast on the sight of them. My dear grandmother, Arabella, sat in the front row with a tiny baby, still red-faced from the womb. I smiled when I heard Roxy's indignant cry. She didn't seem to mind she was interrupting the Supreme Court. If she was uncomfortable, everyone was going to know it.

Arabella, flushed and beautiful in her new mother look, bounced tiny Roxy. All the force of the stars flashed in the baby's dark eyes until they closed, and she gave a little sigh of resignation. Arabella's sigh was from relief.

Eli had gone forward and been shown to the high court's seat of testimony.

"You are here to speak to the character, or lack thereof, of the defendant, Leona Koenig."

A hovering display of news articles, facts and schematics, transparent to the outside viewers but visible to Eli, surrounded him in the defendant's chair. He brought up the schematic of the wormhole within the portal cap.

"Leona Koenig was assigned to the research facility because of her exceptional grasp of electromagnetic technology and the brilliance she displayed in her physics classes. We are not trying to disprove her intelligence or her contributions to the CAP project today. We are establishing evidence for the formal accusation initiated by the Director of Science within the ministry of New York, Arabella Eisen. You are here because of your work on that project," the judge clarified.

"I understand." Eli nodded as he studied the representation of the damage done to the portal.

"You are mentioned in the accusation as an eyewitness to the crime." The judge, clad in the simple garb of every other member of the time, held a gavel in her hand, which seemed to be only for effect.

"I was there."

"Please give us your version of events."

Eli sighed and glanced at Arabella. "Leona was upset. Arabella found the formula to initiate time travel within the portal cap first, and Leona didn't think it was fair."

"Objection. Conjecture." The defense attorney interrupted.

The judge nodded at Eli. "Go ahead."

Eli continued. "Leona became increasingly irate, though she

hid her feelings from the rest of the research team. When I came in one evening to record daily diagnostics on the portal – temperature, stability, things like that – I noticed the stability was lower than it had ever been and the temperature was high. Only the three of us have access to the portal cap, to limit the possibility of someone causing damage. I had a feeling Leona had done something to get back at us.

"The security monitoring system had been shut down, but I was able to repair it enough to find a few images from the night in question." Eli brought up the footage and enlarged it to hover in the center of the room for everyone to see. Leona, dressed in black and throwing a defiant glance toward the door, cranked the lever that controlled temperature. Immediately the portal light intensified and anything in the room not bolted down or prepared for the reaction was sucked inside. This included two scientists.

"And to be clear – who are you identifying on this footage?" the judge asked.

"Leona Koenig." Eli glanced at her with a sigh that told the room he was sorry to have to name her.

"What is your relationship to Leona Koenig?" another judge asked as he replayed the footage again.

"Friends," Eli said. "Since college. The three of us had similar classes and interests. We fed off each other's intellectual energy."

"There was never anything more than friendship between the two of you?"

Eli hesitated. Leona narrowed her eyes at him. He swallowed, as if in pain.

"She's hurting him," Jamie whispered.

"I know." I nodded.

Eli went on, despite the pain. "She hinted that she wanted there to be more between the two of us. But there was never anyone for me but Arabella."

"Do you think you are the reason she committed this crime?"

Eli looked sad. "I think Leona wants to be in control more

than anything else. I think she feels this was missing from her childhood, and she is searching for a way to be on top. That Arabella has constantly held the position higher than Leona, and that I fell in love with Arabella instead of her..." Eli's voice trailed off for a moment.

"I think it's causing her to escalate her agenda to get to the top in any way she can. That's why Leona claims Arabella's faulty calculations caused those scientists to die when they went through the portal. In her heart, I can believe Leona wants that to be the truth, even though she's the one who caused the incident."

They dismissed him. The way he painfully stumbled back to his seat and the intense concentration I read in Leona's expression told me he was paying for his honest answers.

I had to give him credit for standing up to her. No one else would. Not when they realized what she could do to those who got in her way.

Seventeen

October 5, 2058

Next, Jamie and I went to the research facility again, almost a year after Leona's hearing. I knew my way around by now. I think Jamie felt the same as we headed for the portal room, high above the immense entryway of the old library.

But when we reached the portal room, we were in unfamiliar territory. I'd learned about it in my studies, and I knew the general layout and everything that happened in that place, but being there was different. I had a sense of foreboding as we came down the hallway. I imagined I could smell the blood before we turned the corner. I felt the electric rays of the portal sending out the signal of doom.

"Eli," I breathed, stopping short and leaning back behind the entrance. I grabbed Jamie before she turned the corner.

"We can't interrupt this," I said, though it killed me to wait outside. The tension and grief was thick in the air. I heard an anguished sob from my grandmother Arabella, and it nearly tore my heart in half.

"Are you sure?" Jamie stared at me with wide eyes as she picked up on the desperation.

"It's an Unalterable." I gritted my teeth and wondered why my mother would subject me to this memory.

"You didn't have to kill him!" I'd never heard Arabella speak so angrily. Leona stood across from her, eyeing the knife in her hand. Her eyes were wide, dazed, as if she had just toppled over some precipice into insanity.

"I didn't," she disagreed, but her voice was high and strange.

I watched Arabella's face as she worked to control her response. She turned and picked up her baby girl from the floor behind her. She held her protectively to her chest, but Roxy didn't understand what was going on and protested at being held so securely. Arabella slowly stepped back, away from Leona.

Before Arabella could get the baby out of the way, Leona suddenly reached out and snatched little Roxy from Arabella's grasp. Roxy started wailing as Leona held the baby by the arm, near the lightning buzz of the portal.

"Lee, I understand you are angry," Arabella said. Her throat sounded thick with terror, but she kept it under control. "It may be you have the right, though I wish you'd said something sooner. I ask one thing – in the name of friendship."

Leona stared at Arabella with a hollow expression as she pushed Roxy closer.

"No!" Arabella cried out, holding up her hands. "Please – just take me instead. She can't hurt you. She's just a baby. I should be the one to go into the portal. Take me instead."

We all held our breath as Leona considered the request. "You deserve this, Bell. You took everything from me."

Arabella didn't answer. She took a careful step forward and slowly reached out to take Roxy back.

"Please." Arabella took another step.

Leona considered her as if she was watching something happening in a dream. Finally, she stood taller and steeled her jaw. "Only one of us can rule."

But a few moments later, Leona released Roxy to Arabella's

arms without explanation. Arabella quickly took the toddler back to the edge of the room, near where we sat spying on the scene. She set Roxy on the chair and scanned the area. Her eyes fell on a young boy hiding behind the long console at the side of the room.

"Who's that?" Jamie whispered.

"My father." I felt a lump in my throat.

Arabella gave Levi a little nod. Then her eyes trailed to the doorway and she looked straight at me. At first, she was surprised. She narrowed her eyes, as if trying to figure out who I was, but at the same time I could see she recognized me.

"Time's up," Leona called in a formidable *I'm going to take over New York City and you can't stop me* tone.

Arabella met my eyes again, desperate. She took a deep breath and looked purposefully at her baby, and then focused on the one hiding under the console. I understood the message as I let my mind open and read hers.

Please make sure they get out safely.

Though I felt a surge of protectiveness for my grandmother, I reminded myself that she would survive her trip through the portal. The little ones would have a harder time escaping Leona's wrath. As I saw out of the corner of my eye one of my grandmothers pushing the other one into the bright abyss, I quickly went for the hiding boy under the console while I motioned for Jamie to grab the baby.

We grabbed the kids and ran. The hiss of the portal followed us all the way down the stairs to the front hall.

I kneeled down in front of a little boy who would one day grow up to be my father. "Do you know what to do now?"

I prayed he did, because I had no idea how my parents had escaped that night.

His eyes were wide and scared, but he nodded. He resolutely took the little chain from the baby girl's neck and pressed a button on its underside. He took her hand and half-led, half-carried the future love of his life to safety. She toddled beside him and tried to keep up with him. They disappeared into the night.

"Seize them!" I heard Leona call from the top of the stairs, pointing at Jamie and me. Guards ran toward us, but I entered our next coordinates and put my arms around Jamie, and we faded out of time.

We came back in the same spot. Which was kind of a problem because the building had been remodeled. Not to mention it seemed like a bad time to make an appearance on the polished marble floors opening to the new courtyard, flooded with citizens.

The atmosphere had changed. Oppression had taken over. A massive crowd of people stood behind roped off sections of the courtyard and a crimson carpet flowed down the stairs like a trail of blood oozing from the portal.

Trumpets began to play an introduction. I suspected we were in the direct path of the newly crowned Regal Manager.

I grabbed Jamie's hand and jumped back. We got behind the rope just as a group of perfectly synchronized soldiers raised laser rifles equipped with antiquated bayonets high into the air.

It was then that I noticed the building. Instead of the old public library, a new structure made of iron and glass seemed to regally rise out of the ground with opened arms that did a formal dance toward the sky.

"Whoa."

Jamie glanced at me. We looked down and saw red. Red hair elegantly arranged in a style from another time, a red dress with more flounce and frill than I'd ever seen in my life.

Servant girls in long black skirts and striped silk blouses carried the long train of Leona's gown. She walked with her chin held high, her welcoming smile a cruel irony.

The trumpets went silent. The crowd was still and quiet. No need to shush anyone. No children cheered or ran; no adults even whispered. Everyone was as silent as the grave.

"My dear, dear people," Leona began, her voice musical and mesmerizing. "How I have waited for this new day of victory and peace to dawn!"

No one met her eyes. The crowd seemed awed and afraid. No one shared her smiles or her joy. She didn't appear to mind.

"They've just survived the Resistance Riots," I whispered to Jamie. "Almost a fourth of the city was killed or sent through the portal by Leona's forces when they tried to go against her setting up her regime."

"We will forget the offenses you have caused in the past," Leona said, waving a delicate hand as if she were the picture of generosity. "I am a loving ruler, and you will see that under my care, our city will flourish and be a place where no one is afraid to go out into the street at night, and every child has enough food to eat. I promise you we will become a beacon in a world that has gone dark in so many ways. We will stand out as those who expand and revolutionize technology. No one will dare to come against us with the power of the portal behind me. I have the ability to destroy any enemy, and I promise I will uphold justice within our city and without."

She paused to give them a prim smile. "We will have a system that works because it will follow order and reason. Rules will be obeyed and lawbreakers dealt with immediately. As long as you conform to the standards of this government, you will have nothing to fear.

"I am your leader because I have conquered the limitations of time and space. I have gone to the past, and seen the order maintained in a different time. I am inspired to repeat the ways of that great age and bring its light to our present circumstances. My government will reflect these principles, and my rewards wait for those who are compliant and helpful to this new age. Go forth, my people, and be better than the rest. We will not settle for average any longer. We will be the strongest, the best, and we will own this world for the sake of our children and our children's children."

As she said the words, one of the servant women brought forward a little boy, dressed exactly like the military generals. He stood in front of Leona and gave a military salute to the crowd.

"It's my dad." It broke my heart to see him up there, trying so hard to be the son Leona wanted him to be.

"I want to introduce your future king, the heir to my throne. I assure you, he is the direct descendent of a strong general who has led his people to safety in these troubling times. His son will be no exception. There will be no end to this dynasty. It will only become stronger, and all the rulers that come after us will take care of you. You must trust us with your absolute allegiance, and you will have the life you thought you could only imagine." Her gaze grew severe as she surveyed the crowed. "But those who fight me will quickly regret it."

There was a long silence. After some time, the servants around Leona began to drop to their knees and bow toward Leona and little Levi.

Eventually, the crowd caught on. They all began to bow. I could feel the moment all of their spirits gave in. They'd bow or face Leona's unknown portal.

I could start a revolution right there in the plaza of the citadel. I could assure the people the portal was not a tool of torture and death. I could go through it and show them.

I suppose that was the moment I understood what my grandmother had been trying to explain my whole life. That just because I *could* do something didn't mean I *should*. As the keeper of time, I had a responsibility to hold the delicate matters of lives gently. Not to interfere in certain moments. To let the difficulties cause the great to emerge from their shells.

I would not handle matters of time and space by force or by gaining absolute control. I would leave a light touch and interfere only with the moments revealed to me. The magnitude of it made me lightheaded. I didn't know how I would pull it off, but I must.

For all of these souls and those that would follow them, I must accomplish the ultimate goal. I would save my ancestors. I would reason it out, make a plan and stick to it.

The soldiers followed Leona and Levi back into the castle of iron and glass and time portal. She waved and smiled. Only a few seemed bold enough to meet her eyes. Even fewer smiled.

A formidable looking man in severe military dress stepped forward and waved so that a hologram of words appeared behind him.

"All citizens of New York presently abiding here shall remain, under penalty of the portal. No one may leave the city. All citizens shall follow dress regulations, under penalty of the portal. All citizens will remain celibate until marriage, and will apply to the government for permission to marry. No one may be joined without approval from the Regal Manager's marriage division. Violators will face the portal. No one may procreate without testing and approval from the government. All cases of illegitimate children will be investigated. All citizens will submit to the placing of a biochip that will monitor your health, your taxes and your adherence to the regulations set forth today. You will proceed to your precinct's clinic to receive this implant within the week or face prosecution by means of the portal.

"Finally, no citizen of this government may under any circumstances question any of these laws. Those of a mind to resist will do well to consider the outcome of the riots, and remember the blood of the rebels that flowed in these very streets over the last year."

She left abruptly, leaving the rules digitally hovering over the crowd as a warning. After the gates of the Crystal Citadel closed, the military forces began to force everyone off the premises.

I watched them go. Defeated and broken, they would now be subject to the whims of Leona's delusions of grandeur. It would be a hard road and a dark time.

I took Jamie's hand and pressed the button on my timeband.

Eighteen

June 21, 2060
Border at Old Lincoln Tunnel

After the next jump, as soon as we came to our senses, we had to run for cover. I'd known we were heading into a volatile situation from the history I'd learned as a child. It was the final Resistance. The one that had killed all the parents of the bunker kids.

We didn't stay long. It was brutal, watching the Citadel peace implementers go after the brave dissenters—men, women, mostly unarmed, standing bravely with hands joined across the bridge, singing the old national anthem of America as the soldiers came at them.

The violence was senseless. Instead of killing them quickly with laser rifles, the soldiers went after them with bayonets, as if their orders had been to leave an impression by shedding more blood than was imaginable.

Jamie was shoving away tears when I took her hand and we headed into the city.

It took a while to find Lafayette Street. It was after curfew, so we had to stay in the shadows. I was glad for the long walk. We were both silent, lost in the impressions of what we had just seen. Our hands clasped together as if someone might try to tear us apart.

"I've seen stuff like that before," Jamie finally whispered. "But I was the one doing it. I *liked* the power. I didn't get what I was doing – until today."

I nodded. "You were brainwashed by Joe. It's not your fault."

She shrugged, but I could tell she didn't completely accept my words.

"Where are we going?" She changed the subject.

"My mom said to go to the secret bunker on Lafayette Street across from the old Astor Library."

She nodded, and we were quiet again until we found the location. It took a bit of hunting around before we found the door to the bunker and a passageway opened into the foundation of a crumbling old theater.

"This place is hidden well."

I nodded, remembering all the facts I'd learned about the bunker when I was younger. "It's hidden by invisibility tech. Made to look like something else, when in fact this entire block is the bunker that will keep my mother safe for the next sixteen years."

"Wow."

I saw the heavy steel circular door at the end of the passage and wondered how in the world we would get in. But when I pressed my hand to the recognition pad, it turned green and the lock disengaged.

"It knows you." Jamie pointed to the hologram above the computer that listed my full name. I frowned. I'd never heard before that I'd had anything to do with the bunker years.

Suddenly, I didn't want to go inside. I had a feeling I was about to learn something about my future. Maybe it was something I wouldn't like. Whatever it was, it was going to change my life.

"The only way to figure out what your mom wanted you to know about this night is to go in and see what she wants you to see," Jamie said sensibly. I sighed and stepped forward, bending down to pass through the entrance.

We came into a long, plain hallway. To the left I saw a control room of sorts, equipped with transparent computer tech. I liked the set-up. It seemed like something I would have come up with.

Down the hall I could see a darkened cafeteria and an opening to an outdoor space that had gardens and natural light coming through. It got my wheels turning, wondering how it worked and energized by the prospect of coming up with tech that could bring the outdoors to an underground bunker.

To the right was a hallway with a single door on the right side. The left side seemed to open up into some kind of arched entrance to a communal room. We heard the sound of sniffles and children. A man's voice spoke.

"It's going to be okay. I'm here to take care of you."

It took me a moment to realize where I'd heard the voice before. Jamie tugged on my arm. "That's *you*."

I gulped as I stepped forward and peeked around the corner. Indeed, it was me, though a much older version. I had baby Roxy in my lap. Other young children surrounded me, their eyes fixed on me as if I was their only hope.

"Will mommy and daddy ever come back?" a little girl of four or five asked him in nothing more than a whisper. I watched my older self reach a palm to the girl's cheek.

"No, baby. I'm sorry. But I'll be your daddy now."

She tried to stifle her sobs, but big tears flowed from her large blue eyes and she sniffed loudly. She managed a nod.

"We're going to have to live smart, kids. I'm going to need your help. We're going to plant in our gardens and take care of our animals. We're going to study and read and learn about history and science. We're going to make music and cook good food and we're going to learn what it means to be a family."

"I don't know how to do any of those things," a boy said in a worried tone.

"It's okay. I do. And I'll teach you. I've been getting ready for this my whole life, and I know exactly what we need to do."

I nodded. And as I did, I saw the older version of me look up and find my eyes, as if he knew I was standing there. He smiled.

"Don't worry. You'll figure out what you are supposed to do. You know the next right step." He seemed to be speaking to the kids, but I knew he was also talking to me.

I was a little creeped out by the fatherly reminder from... me, so I turned and abruptly headed down the hallway, Jamie in tow. When I remembered I had the ability to manipulate time, I fumbled for my timeband and pressed the button.

The next place in the queue was also in the bunker, a few years later. We came out of the time stream standing in exactly the same spot in the hallway in front of the steel entrance door.

The place was different, but the same. It was no longer unused, so it had wear on the trim and scuffs on the floor. The children that had sat around older me nine years before scurried here and there doing their jobs with excited giggles and loud conversations.

An alarm sounded, and the bunker immediately went quiet, except for the shuffling of feet as everyone made their way to their quarters for the night. The lights in the hall automatically dimmed and soft classical piano played quietly.

We walked to the back of the bunker and followed the path outside to the gardens. I wanted to see how they were set up. It was beginning to become clear to me that I was the one who was going to build this bunker, so I wanted to at least have a basic understanding of what they were going to need. I knew about invisibility tech, and I could see how the bunker was hidden, but I wanted to know the specifics.

I was amazed as I walked into their courtyard space. Solar lamps gave it a soft glow. I saw tomato plants and cucumbers, some sort of fruit tree, long, golden stalks of wheat and cornstalks towering over the rest of the plants. Across the path of pea gravel grew beans, peas, and lettuces. A raised bed provided an array of herbs, some clearly medicinal. I was going to make notes in my timeband computer, but a voice from behind me made me whirl around.

"Don't worry about the particulars. You'll figure it out."

I laughed, but not because I thought the situation was funny. I couldn't believe I was standing there talking to myself.

"This is probably the weirdest thing I've ever seen." Jamie stared at my face, then moved closer to study his. "How can the same person be standing in the same room as two versions of himself? Time travel is crazy."

The older Morris suddenly went misty-eyed as Jamie spoke, and he came to her, arms outstretched. He took Jamie's hands and stared into her face with intensity that made me feel a little jealous, which was ridiculous. She went silent, staring back.

"Jamie," he breathed, shaking her hands as if he wanted to embrace her, but didn't want to scare her. "You're here. I've been waiting for this – to see you again."

Suddenly, I had an uncomfortable feeling. I was all for looking into the past. I wanted to understand where I'd come from and fix the broken spots in our story. But I wasn't so sure I wanted to look into the future. I wasn't sure I should. I swallowed hard, trying not to imagine why I would be staring at Jamie that way in twenty years, like I hadn't seen her in forever. Like I'd lost her.

Jamie caught on, too. She frowned and her eyes darted wildly to meet my gaze.

Older Morris seemed to understand we were uncomfortable. He squeezed her hands and cleared his throat. "It's okay. Really. Don't worry. There are two ways to look at everything."

He didn't offer an explanation. I didn't want one.

"Mom sent you here?" He let her go and turned to me, though I could tell he didn't want to release Jamie's hands. His thoughts were crystal clear in my mind. I couldn't have blocked them if I tried. Not too surprising, considering he was me.

"Yes. I'm not completely sure why yet. I think she wants me to see the timeline so I can figure out what needs to change."

He nodded, but he was thoughtful. "I wouldn't say *change*. I'd say *modify*, kind of like you'd adjust a lens for perspective and clarity."

I was skeptical, and I'm sure he could see it.

He studied me. "You know about Unalterables already, don't you?"

"Grandma talks about them. She says some points are fixed in time. If you tried to change them, you'd only end up causing them to happen."

He nodded slowly. "You need to be careful. Don't adjust the past to suit yourself. Don't do it out of charity. Do it because if you don't, we'll never get to the end. It's about survival."

"You mean I shouldn't save anyone?" I was confused. Wasn't it my duty to save the past?

"Save if it makes things better for the Transient people." He chose the words carefully, as if he was trying to say something without giving something else away.

I shrugged. "I guess I'll figure it out along the way."

He nodded and glanced again at Jamie.

There are two perspectives for everything.

"Is Roxy here?" I looked around, but the halls had gone silent.

"Where else would she be?" He grinned, and he motioned to the control room. We walked the hall to get there, and I leaned in to see a girl of about ten with wild dark hair and flashing eyes staring at a computer monitor with intense frustration. I could see by the set of her pursed mouth and her rigid stance, as if ready for attack, that she was the same Roxy I knew. Though I didn't know her well enough. I felt wistful staring at the little girl who would become my mother in less than ten years.

"Why are your feelings so mushy?" Roxy made a sound of disgust and shot a glare my way. I chuckled.

She whirled around. I could see by her expression she didn't know I was a different version of her caretaker. "What? Why are you staring at me, Morris?"

I shook my head and was about to speak when elder Morris spoke into my mind.

Watch your words. She doesn't know who we are yet.

I was surprised, but it made sense. Telling my ten-year-old mother I was her son was probably not the best use of my time traveling skills.

"Hey, Roxy. You get to bed soon." I tried my hand at sounding authoritative.

She made a face. "I'm going, I'm going. I'm almost finished with my report on the citadel rules. I can't believe the nerve of Leona! Telling people what to wear and who to marry! What a load of propaganda this is! I'd like to march right up to that silly palace of hers and give her a piece of my mind. Or maybe just my fist." She held up her fist for illustration, and I was convinced no one had ever been as adorable as my mother, Roxy Eisen, as a child.

I drank in the sight of her before I ducked out and turned back to Jamie and Morris.

"I think we're ready to go," I said, though part of me wanted to stay.

"What's next on her list?" Morris asked.

"June 21, 2074." I read the date from my timeband.

"Ah. You know that date."

I tried to remember the significance of the date. The place was once again the portal room at the citadel.

"Just like me. Forgetting the answers to my tests as soon as I was done taking them. Go on, then, but be careful. You're going to want to stay in the background on this one. If I remember correctly, I almost got myself portaled."

"Good to know." I stared at him, wishing I could stay for a few days, at least, and find out everything he already knew that had to do with my mission.

His gaze softened. "You don't need anything else from me right now. You're exactly where you're supposed to be."

I nodded, cleared my throat and reached for Jamie's hand before we faded out.

Nineteen

"Am I to assume that Miss Eisen captured you and removed your tracker, General Koenig?"

It was the first thing I heard, coming from Leona's mouth, when we awkwardly appeared in the hallway outside the portal room. We quickly moved out of sight.

Levi only answered her with a defiant stare.

"That's exactly what happened," Roxy said, but neither of them seemed to remember she was standing there.

"Let Roxy go," Levi said. "You have no reason to hold her."

His mind screamed though his voice was quiet. I sensed strong emotion on either side. His rage and Leona's injury. She wanted him to pay for his betrayal.

Her chilling eyes looked at Roxy. The corners of her painted mouth turned up, but she wasn't smiling. "You murdered a security guard, Roxanne. Do you see how far you've fallen? What you've resorted to in your ill-advised little rebellion? What choice have you left me? You're a killer who has endangered hundreds of children."

Leona moved closer to Roxy. "You made my decision for me. Just like your mother. The guilty pay for their crimes."

Roxy scoffed. "What about your crimes? What about how you

murdered my parents? Shouldn't you pay for that?"

Leona was disdainful, but if I hadn't imagined it, a tremor of weakness burrowed somewhere within her being. Roxy seemed to sense it and pushed further.

"I've heard the whole story. How you hated my mom because she got everything you thought you deserved. I heard how you killed my father because he didn't love you, and you pushed my mom in the portal." Roxy sneered at her. "Did she beg for her life?"

Leona's expression darkened by volumes.

"She didn't, did she? I bet she gave her life for me. You wanted to kill me to hurt her. That sounds like the Regal Manager we know."

Leona roared with anger. "Brand her!"

Soldiers held Roxy down. Levi rushed toward her, but with one motion of Leona's wrist he was captured by two more soldiers and held back. Roxy twisted her neck so she could see him. His eyes were wide with anguish as he struggled against them. In that moment I realized just how connected my parents had always been to each other. I had come from that connection. It was a part of me. In a sense, it *was* me.

Roxy screamed in pain at the same time I heard Levi's desperate cry inside my mind. Veins protruded from his forehead as his face turned purple. He fought frantically to free himself.

"You're crazy! You're evil! I promise I will kill you if you don't let her go NOW!" The words tore from his throat as if he had no control over them. Leona turned to him, hurt.

I'd never seen Levi so raw and unfiltered. The mad swirl of words that erupted from his mind was saturated with disillusionment. It was the feeling of a little boy who'd been turned out of his own house.

Levi, she's not worth this pedestal you have her on.

I distinctly heard my mother's silent words, speaking to Levi. His eyes found hers and he couldn't stop the thought fast enough.

She should be. A mother should be.

It must have been the first time Roxy realized who Leona was to Levi. Her mind reeled with the news.

The soldiers dragged Roxy toward the access doors as they opened, while Leona tried to soothe Levi in a musical voice. The sound was a contradiction. I felt her emotions and there was nothing compassionate or nurturing in them, only hate. She wanted Roxy dead.

"You know I love you," she murmured over him. "Everything I do is for you. She's manipulating you, baby. Can't you see that?"

He backed away from her reaching hands and scowled. "You're unbelievable. You make the people of this city believe you are their savior and take everything from them to give yourself more. You're a coward. You hide behind your portal and kill anyone who dares to stand up to you." He stood taller. "People like you never win in the end. The heroes are always the ones like Roxy."

The guards paused, unsure of their orders. They shifted and pretended not to be witness to the scene.

Levi took a step toward Leona. "I'm standing up to you now. I've tried to believe the best about you, but you make it impossible. Are you going to portal me, too?"

She glared, barely maintaining her composure. Fury colored the space around her. "You need to be very careful, Levi."

Levi shook off the hold of the guards and came to Roxy.

"If you send Roxy into the portal, I'm going with her."

"So be it!" Leona's face contorted. "Go with your sorceress. You are *nothing* to me. No true son of mine would choose her over me. Throw her in!"

The guards, looking terrified, moved quickly to obey. Roxy started to panic, breathing fast and calling Levi's name in little gasps as the magnetic pull of the swirl reached for her with hungry, powerful fingers.

"Hold on, Roxy!" Levi called. As she was tossed in and

swallowed up, he closed his eyes and took a deep breath. With the most terrified and the most courageous expression I'd ever seen on anyone's face, he took a flying leap into all that light and disappeared.

We didn't have any time to linger. I set my timeband and we left.

September 27, 2074
Crystal Citadel, the portal

"We're in the same place," Jamie said, confused. Indeed, the portal room looked exactly as it had before, only it was empty. The portal spurted and sputtered as if it was protesting a massive amount of use. I could feel power humming off it. For some reason, the whole of the portal felt like my mother. Roxy seemed to be present like a spirit, haunting it like a ghost.

"It's three months later," I explained to Jamie. "They've come back from 1874. This is the night they take the Citadel."

I realized what was about to happen in that room and I ushered Jamie into a supply closet where we could watch without being a part of the showdown that was about to occur.

Leona ran into the room, breathing fast as if she had been running all night. She stood next to the portal, her cold eyes watching the door like a trapped animal.

"Going somewhere, Leona?" Roxy stepped into the room with her rifle propped against her shoulder.

Not only did I feel it, but I clearly saw fear flash across Leona's features. There was jealousy and hatred, but mostly, there was fear.

We heard a voice crackle over the com. "Citizens of New York City, what happens in the portal chamber today will determine our future. Watch your queen dethroned."

A haunting cheer echoed through the palace.

"You know how this will end," Roxy said.

Fear multiplied in the space around Leona like hysterical icy sparks darting into the air. But she stuck out her chin and scoffed.

"You're just a child," she said.

"You stole the freedom of this city. Today, we take it back."

"I wanted to help them," Leona said in a fragile tone.

"You really believe that?" Roxy asked, but we both knew she did. It made me feel pity for my grandmother who had made her own life so hard.

"I've taken care of you all for sixteen years. Just like a mother caring for her children."

Roxy shook her head with a humorless chuckle. "I've seen the way you mother your child. You suck at it."

Leona stood up straight. "You're just a girl. His latest conquest. You can never compete with his mother."

She stood taller, and her eyes narrowed into slits. I knew Leona was using her power on Roxy when I saw Roxy inhale quickly and go rigid.

Fight it, I urged her silently. *People can only have as much control over you as you allow.*

"Cut it out, or I shoot." Roxy snarled. She propped the rifle into position and put her finger on the trigger. "Now."

Leona leaned back against the console as if the attempt to subdue Roxy had cost her something. I read pain and saw the flash of it in her eyes.

Then we heard them. Out on the streets, within the halls of the palace, a cry rose loud and strong for quick and final resolution. Justice was demanded for the tyrant who cowered in front of Roxy.

Roxy held the trigger. *I'll give the people what they want.* But she hesitated. *Mom and Levi loved her.*

Her finger slipped away from the trigger.

Levi was standing in the doorway. He met my eyes, but when he saw the gun pointed at Leona, he stepped into the portal room.

"Roxy –"

In the moment it took her to glance at him, to hear what he had to say, Leona took a leap toward the portal.

And disappeared.

Twenty

December 26, 1776
Outside Trenton, New Jersey

I wasn't surprised by the date of the next jump, because it was familiar as my own reflection in the mirror. It was my birthday. My *actual* birthday. But as I stood in the nearly pitch-black forest with freezing rain biting my face, I realized that my birth had been no simple matter.

"Do you know why we're here?" Jamie whispered in the still of the forest.

The silence was shred apart by an angry scream of frustration. I smiled at the sound of Roxy's voice. "This is the night I was born."

I saw an abandoned shed with no door and moved forward, holding Jamie's hand so I didn't lose her in the darkness. As we peered into the shed lit only with the pale haze of the winter storm, I saw my father carrying Roxy in his arms. He set her down and took off his Revolutionary rebel military coat, laid it on the ground and helped her with her clothes.

"Don't attack it, Roxy. Go with it," I heard Levi suggest as she lay back on the coat.

She turned fierce, wild eyes on him. "You idiot mudsill! This is YOUR fault! If I die it will be YOUR FAULT!"

I snorted and looked at Jamie. She raised an eyebrow but didn't comment.

"That's my mom." I shrugged.

Another contraction took Roxy's breath and she squeezed her eyes shut. When it passed, she kicked Levi so hard he fell back against the wall.

"I hate you! I hate you and I wish you were dead!"

Don't smile. Smile and she'll kill me. I heard my father coaching himself.

But there was the mind-reading obstacle. Roxy heard every word he thought and seethed. "Give me my knife so I can slit your throat!" She added a few more colorful words.

In the next moment, I realized why my mother wanted me to see this. I stood in awe and watched as my father gathered my mother's face in his hands and bent his forehead against hers, because suddenly the sight of her enduring such a huge act of love on behalf of both of them made him love her more than he ever had before.

"I'm so sorry, Rox. I wish I could fix this. I would do it for you if I could. You are so strong. So strong and beautiful, and you're doing great."

She cried out again and grabbed his knee so hard he bit his lip to keep back his own yell. She steeled herself and pushed with a power I'd never witnessed before. I was in awe as much as Levi was.

As she gasped for air, another cry joined hers. I watched myself enter the world, gasping for air on my father's rebel jacket.

Levi picked up the squirming, slippery mass in his arms.

It's a boy. I'm holding my son. I'm a father.

As I watched them, I felt an undeniable sense of guilt creep over me. I had wanted nothing more than my parents my entire childhood. I had chafed that I had to stay in the Transient village with my grandmother instead of be with them where they lived deep in the past. I had doubted they even loved me. I had thought, only to myself, of course, that they couldn't have cared about me that much if they were willing to give me up.

But here they were, tears shining in their eyes, tender glances shared with each other. Levi gently handed me to my mother. Roxy held me as if I was made of glass and would break if she did something wrong. She gasped with emotion as she looked back at Levi.

They didn't need to speak. I could hear the thoughts swirling in both their heads. It didn't take words to see it anyway. Love hovered around them, warming the chilly night air with something that promised to be stronger than the cold, than the war, than the doubts and questions of two young people who were in a rough spot and had no idea what to do next. They didn't realize they had everything they needed. They had love.

I felt as if I'd suddenly done a whole lot of growing up in a very short amount of time. I squeezed Jamie's hand and reluctantly pressed the button on my timeband. Part of me wanted to stay there in that moment for as long as it lasted, and feast upon the sight of my parents loving me. I'd missed that feeling so many times during my childhood.

But a bigger part of me wanted to press on. To see the last place Roxy wanted me to go, and witness the last event in the time sequence she felt was important for me to know firsthand. Then I would take all the experiences she had armed me with and go home and make a plan.

A plan to save my people.

January 25, 1777
Central Park area, New York City

The last of the sun disappeared on the horizon as Jamie and I came through behind a collection of black rock and oak trees. I saw my mother immediately. Roxy was holding the baby and staring into the sky as if it held the answer to her dilemma.

Please show me the way. You're stars. It's what you do – lead the way home.

"Roxy?" I heard my father's voice.

She looked up, her face a desperate mix of hope and despair.

"Levi." She looked at him with tears in her eyes. He kneeled beside her and put his hand on the baby's – on my – soft brown hair. I heard the baby grunt in contentment. He was glad Levi had come. Glad our family was together.

Roxy watched Levi. "What's wrong?"

I saw the telltale signs of sorrow in Levi's face. "She's dead."

She didn't answer right away. "Leona?"

He nodded. I felt it with him – the sting of the tears that wanted to fall. His mother was dead. My grandmother was dead.

"Did you...?"

He shook my head. "Joe killed her."

"I'm sorry, Levi," she whispered.

"She died for me, Roxy," Levi explained. "She could have saved herself, but she saved me instead."

I felt Roxy's surprise. She didn't answer. She just held his cheek with her palm and watched him.

"How did you know you should leave Trenton?" Levi asked.

"Joe's coming," she said dully. "I feel it as strong as I felt you getting close. He's nearby. He's taunting me. He's going to hurt the baby."

"Your feeling was right. He is coming after you." Levi lifted his shirt and showed her a scar and blood stains. "But he tried to hurt me and failed, thanks to your mom."

She touched the scar. "I'm glad you're okay."

Levi stared into her eyes. I read his thoughts greedily, like a starved man handed a plate of food. Levi considered all her imperfection so perfectly measured together with a brand of goodness she shouldn't have, given her history with pain and struggle. He couldn't stop the words from tumbling forth, even though he was afraid she wouldn't want to hear it.

"I love you."

Her eyes searched his. Even her thoughts were speechless. She felt treasured. She felt honored. She felt the same.

Her fingers traced his jawline. "There should be something stronger. Some word or gesture. Then I could express it." Her voice was a whisper as loud as time, wrapping its fingers tight on our souls. *It's the measure of us. The measure of Levi and Roxy and their son. Time has tested us in ways we didn't expect, and here we are, in the middle of a war inside a war, and time has not been able to conquer it – the love that breathes and lives in the space between us.*

Levi held them both, and kissed her with silent words that insisted on climbing out of his thoughts and reaching into hers. They barely noticed the light at first. But it became brighter until all the shadows we were hiding in had been swallowed up. And even before I looked toward the light, I knew what it was. Because it had come from the same time manipulator that had brought us to this place.

"Good grief!" Jamie gasped. "There's *three* of you here!"

Another Morris stepped out of the light that seemed a doorway to nothing. He gave them a long look of apology, even as he stared at them in awe, just as I had been doing.

Morris eventually found his words. "I'm so sorry, Roxy. Levi. I need to take your son."

Roxy stared at Levi in desperation. *Giving him up would be the same as ripping out my heart and handing it over.*

Levi grabbed her arms and held them both close. "I know, babe."

Please tell me there's another way, she begged.

"Joe is close," Morris confirmed what Roxy had felt and Levi had known. He eyed his timeband on his arm, not very different from the one I was wearing. "Joe has tech you should know about.

Leona brought a teleportation device. As soon as he figures out how to use it, he'll be standing next to us. We won't have any warning."

Levi looked at Roxy. "You know I would never try to force you to give up our baby. But as his father, I'm telling you, I can't keep him safe here. Deep down, you know you can't, either."

She choked back a sob that reminded me of the dying soldiers on the battlefield. Other Morris came closer and held a hand to the back of her head. He watched her in peace.

"I promise you both – your son will live. He'll be fine. You just need to trust me and let me take him."

"How can I just give him to you? I don't know where you came from. I don't know where you'll take him. Why can't I go with you?" Roxy resisted.

"It's not the right time. There is more you need to do. Get back to Sophie. She'll take you where you need to go." Morris kneeled next to her and held out his arms for the baby, who cooed in contentment. "Roxy, I raised you. You know you can trust me. Let me take him to safety."

Roxy searched her son's features as if she was memorizing every detail of his perfect baby face. He reached a fist to bat at her hair.

"I can't," she whispered. Morris smiled, the palm of his hand sliding down to her cheek.

"I know you can, Roxy. I know it because you already did."

I found myself nodding. Jamie looked at me and her mouth turned upward in a half-grin. It was important – this moment. I knew why Roxy had sent me here last. She wanted me to know it hadn't been easy to give me up. That it had ripped out her heart to do it. And that was exactly what I needed to know.

The tech beside us surged with protest at the amount of power being drained from the surrounding area. Any moment Joe would appear, and the baby would be stolen from her arms before anyone could react. Roxy took a long, ragged breath. But something suddenly caught her eye. She reached to push aside the gathers of Morris' shirt. I saw it, too.

"The mark," Roxy whispered. "You were just branded by Leona at the citadel."

I shook my head, frowning. Jamie glanced at me. I put my hand to my chest and rubbed my skin, free of burn or scar.

"Aw, it's just a scratch," the other Morris said with a shrug.

"That was almost two years ago," she said, touching the wound. He winced. Levi reached for him and healed the wound.

Morris smiled at Levi. "Thanks." He looked back at Roxy. "For me, it was about ten minutes ago. Which is why I had to cut this so close. I'm sorry about that."

"You were just portaled?" Levi asked, and other Morris nodded.

"Technically. But I have ways to control the wormhole."

"Who are you?" Roxy said the words like she knew exactly who he was, but couldn't accept the truth. But as she stared at him, she suddenly handed the baby to Morris in one quick movement and shuddered at the emotional toll it took to do it.

"Thank you," he said softly to both of them. He stood and turned toward the doorway that seemed to lead to nothing but light.

"Don't worry," he turned around. "I'm taking this guy to the place he needs to be. He'll be fine."

"Will I ever see him again?" Roxy didn't cry. Her breathing was fast and her throat sounded swollen, but she wouldn't give in to the tears. Levi helped her stand.

"You will. You'll have many years together. You'll teach him how to be great, Roxy." Morris's voice had gone very soft and his eyes were misty. "You're going to teach him courage and responsibility. You're going to show him what it means to be a family. He's going to learn all that from you."

"When?"

"When the time is right," Morris said, with all the feeling of someone who knew what he was saying. Like he'd already been there and seen it.

"But how do you know for sure he'll be okay?" Roxy persisted.

Morris watched Roxy fight for control, watched Levi hold her. I knew exactly what he was thinking. He stared at them with emotion spilling over.

"I know he'll be okay, because *I'm* okay."

Time seemed to stand still. None of them spoke.

As if he knew they would have trouble believing it, he held the baby in one arm and used the other hand to unzip and pull apart the gathers of his uniform. Below his branding scar, on his chest, he pointed to a horizontal scar across his heart. Then he patted Baby Morris's chest.

I looked down at my own chest. I knew the scar was there on me. I'd seen it in the mirror many times. And my grandmother had said it was because she had saved my life before I was even born, after I was wounded by a sword of the Revolutionary War.

His time-traveling device hummed to life as he gave me one last look. "I'll see you soon, Dad. Love you, Mom."

Roxy laughed as she gasped a sob, a sound that was exultant and heartbroken, as much a paradox as the sight in front of us. Morris winked as he took a step back into the light.

"Don't believe everything you read in science fiction. This little guy and I have a few minutes before worlds start imploding."

Before he disappeared, he looked over them. Past the trees, into the darkness where he must have known we were standing.

He nodded with a smile before he turned and left.

As darkness covered them like a shroud, I felt Jamie close beside me.

"What now?" she whispered.

I could hear my mother crying and Levi murmuring to her. I wanted to go to them and hold them to me and never let them go. How could I have been so selfish to spend my childhood thinking they didn't love me or didn't want me? Obviously, it had broken their heart when *I* took me away from them.

Some things had to happen. Whether they were ideal or even good, some bad things were part of a grander story that only made sense if they happened.

Unalterables. That was what Grandmother called them.

"I need to go home and make a plan," I said, distracted. She didn't answer, so I held her hand and pressed the button that would send us flying back to our own time.

Twenty-One

"We're home," I said, breathing deeply. 2094 felt clearer. Freer. There was something in all of the other times that made me feel foggy and not quite with it.

"*You're* home." Jamie's voice was morose. I looked at her, my attention stolen by her pretty features that suddenly looked so sad.

I took her hands, suddenly feeling that overwhelming sense of love. I wasn't sure I'd ever felt it before. I knew one thing for sure – I wanted Jamie Salvatore, or Anika Hegemen, or whoever she really was, to be with me for the rest of my life.

"Come with me." My whisper brought her gaze up to mine. Her lower lip trembled.

"Morris," she began, but she stopped and looked down at our tightly joined hands. I didn't want her to say any more. I was afraid she'd say she was leaving me. Instead of listening to her, I took advantage of her hesitation and kissed her as an attempt to tell her – show her – what she really meant to me.

She finally pushed me away and stepped back. "Morris, I don't belong in this world. All I've ever done here is kill and destroy on Joe's behalf."

"That doesn't matter," I said firmly, taking her firmly by the

145

shoulders. "Do you hear me? It doesn't matter where you've been. It matters what is true today. And today, you are no longer a SkyJack who wants to destroy the Transient village. You are Jamie of the past, who wants to learn a new way, who wants to redeem the ancestors, who wants to be part of something that will ensure our survival and our preservation of all the best parts of being alive and being human. You are going to help me save history."

I smiled and allowed an extra infusion of peace to travel through me and reach her. It brought a weak smile to her face, but she still shook her head with apology.

"Morris, that's your job." Her voice was weak and tired.

"It can be yours, too."

"No," she said, shaking her head again.

"Is it Joe? Do you honestly want to go back to the sky dwellers?"

She twisted her mouth. "No. But I'm afraid I might. Joe's been brainwashing me most of my life. I don't know anything different."

"You do now," I said firmly. "You know me. You know I won't let you go back. I want you to stay with me... always."

"I don't think it's possible." She gave a long sigh.

"I need you." I gulped, not sure if I could bring my independent young spirit in line enough to say the words that sat heavy on my tongue, wanting to be said. Needing to be said.

I took a deep breath. "Jamie, I love you. I want you to bond with me."

This brought her eyes back to mine. She raised any eyebrow. "Bond?"

I cleared my throat and looked down. "It's like getting married."

She still frowned as if she didn't understand what I was saying.

"Don't SkyJacks pair off?"

She gave a short laugh. "Not for long."

I searched my brain, trying to find a way to tell her what I wanted us to be. "My parents! That's a good way to put it. I want us to be like my parents."

Understanding dawned. And I could feel her emotions, that she became wistful. She wanted it, too.

"Will you?" I asked softly.

The longest moment of my life happened before she finally answered.

"I'm scared."

I nodded, understanding. I knew what I needed to do.

"How about a bit of insurance?"

She shook her head, confused.

I held up my timeband and let her watch me set it. "Twenty years from today. Let's see what the future holds."

She stared at the projection with wide eyes. "What if it's not good?"

I shrugged. "At least we'll know. Right?"

She held her arms tight across her chest and looked so pale I thought she would refuse, but suddenly, she seemed to find a resolve deep down in her warrior spirit.

"Let's go." She grabbed my hands and held on as if she would die if she let go. I didn't overthink it. I just pressed the button and let gravity take us away.

Transient Village, twenty years later

I looked around the room, which looked the same as my grandmother's, except more worn.

"It's pretty quiet," I whispered. "Let's go outside."

She didn't answer, but she gave a slight nod.

We went down the stairs and walked out the open door. I could smell the bonfire and hear cheerful voices in the village square. But they didn't match the devastation all around us.

"SkyJacks did this," she said in a dull tone. "I knew it wouldn't be good."

"You don't know anything yet," I said. "Give it a chance."

The sound of music and dancing stopped and a voice spoke loudly.

"We honor the Life Giver today for setting us free from our enemy. We honor Morris and Jamie for saving our village and giving us a chance to begin again."

I smirked at Jamie. "There you go."

She relaxed and gave me a small smile. I urged her on and we came to the outer edge of the crowd in the square.

When the cheering died down, Grandma spoke. "Let's have a bonding!"

More cheering followed as two figures stepped forward and stood in front of the bonfire for everyone to see them. They joined hands.

"Do you, Sephora of the Transient, promise to live with Pieter for every day of the rest of your life?" Roxy's voice sounded small in the quiet of the ruined Transient village.

"I promise." The girl held his hands tightly.

"Will you stay with Sophie for the rest of your days?" I felt my heart skip a beat when I heard my mother's voice. Roxy turned to Pieter, a smile playing at the corner of her mouth. Levi stood behind her, his arms around her waist.

"I promise," the young man I assumed was Pieter said in a tone that made it clear he intended to follow through.

"What about when life is hard? When there is work to do, when you feel tired and useless and you wonder if there is something better for you somewhere else? Will you both hold true to your promises today even if you don't feel like it?" Levi asked.

The couple nodded together. "We'll stay together. No matter what."

"What if one of you gets sick or discouraged? Will you stay

by their side and see them through their dark times?"

I searched the crowd for the source of the voice.

"That's you!" Jamie said softly in a relieved voice.

I nodded. "And you."

She looked and saw what I meant, for my elder self held tightly to the hand of a woman who was quite obviously Jamie's older self, beautiful and confident and clothed in the dress of a Transient elder.

"We will." Pieter's determined expression made his eyes flash in the light of the fire. The entire surviving Transient surrounded it, grouped in families, witnessing the bonding ceremony.

The girl, who held a hint of familiarity even though I knew I had never seen her before and indeed would not have been alive in our year of 2094, wore a white dress and a wreath of daisies in her hair.

"My dear little Sephora, my precious girl," Arabella said in nothing more than a whisper. Finally, she found her voice. "Will you both go to any lengths to protect your bond? Will you make it your priority even when other things seem more urgent?"

Sephora nodded, my own tears slipping free at the sight of her dear face. "Yes, Gigi."

I chuckled in disbelief and looked at Jamie to see if she'd figured out who the bride was. She eyed me uncertainly.

"If you are parted by death, as we all know is an all too frequent possibility in this world of survival, will you honor the other's memory? Remember them and share them with your offspring?" Arabella said, her voice catching with emotion.

"Yes," Sephora said softly, and Pieter nodded his agreement.

"Our people take witness." My older, deeper voice spoke with authority. "Today you have bonded. Two as one. Honor your bond with your life, and be happy. Remember love is a choice, not a feeling, and you will do well."

The people applauded the familiar blessing. Older Morris smiled. "Go ahead. Give him a kiss!"

The young woman slid her arms around her new partner's neck as he held her around the waist, and they shared a kiss as the crowd applauded. When they parted, they were hovering in the air above the bonfire. Everyone laughed as Jamie looked at me in wonder. I shrugged.

"Let us celebrate this bond today as we celebrate our new beginning! Dance, eat, and be happy!" Arabella called to everyone, who complied with joy.

As the music started up again and the people began their celebration, I turned to Jamie and raised my eyebrows. I held her hands and stood as close as I could and still look her in the eyes.

"So?"

"So what?" Her cheeks were red as she smiled.

"So that's a bonding."

She nodded. "I get it. But I'd like to know who that girl is."

I looked back at the crowd, seeing the new couple dancing in the middle of the group.

"I think I know."

I wasn't sure. It was a stab in the dark. But putting all the pieces together, and studying the spirit of the girl who had just become part of a bond, I had a pretty good guess.

"I think that's our daughter."

She gasped, her mouth open.

"I'm pretty sure everything turns out okay." I pressed a kiss against her parted lips. "So, will you bond with me? Or are you going back to Joe and the SkyJacks?"

She shrugged and tried to appear nonchalant. "Nah, I guess I'll stay. Love is a choice, right? I guess I'll choose you."

I smiled and kissed her. "I choose you, too."

Jamie looked up to the skies as if she were searching for the SkyJack airships. They were clear. Quiet. She looked back at me. "Looks like you're where I land."

Twenty-Two

I had to make one more stop in time before Jamie and I bonded. The time twenty years in the future seemed like the perfect happy ending, but I had an uncomfortable feeling that it wasn't the end of the story. I left Jamie behind to plan our bonding ceremony with Arabella and snuck off to the future to speak to my mother.

I returned to the bonding ceremony in 2116 again, and stood out in the brush until I had a chance to get my mother's attention. She smiled and came to me. Her face was older, though she couldn't be more than thirty-two or thirty-three. Only the faintest lines had begun to gather around her eyes. Maturity was really the only factor that gave her away. She looked wiser.

"Hi, Morris." She pressed her palm to my cheek. "How old are you?"

"Nineteen."

"Ah. Ready to bond with Jamie."

I nodded. "I went to every place on your list. How did you know where to find all those events?"

She shrugged and gave a little sigh that told me she didn't want to tell me the whole truth. "Levi and I spent a lot of time in the portal bunker in the decade we lived in the past. We got the

151

timeline nailed down. I had a feeling I was the one who helped you discover it."

"You know everything?"

She eyed me suspiciously. "Don't you dare try to get me to tell you things you aren't supposed to know yet, kid."

I smiled. "Wouldn't dream of it. But I'm confused on a couple things."

Roxy shrugged. "Try me. But I'm not promising anything."

"Does Jamie die?"

She stared at me for a long moment. "Yes… and no."

"It can't be both. Either she dies or she doesn't."

"Your council executes her for her BioDroid program when it glitches. But don't try to stop it, Morris. It will be set right later."

"What does that mean?" I wanted her to be more specific. I wanted her to tell me how in the world it could be okay that the love of my life was going to die. How could I just let that happen?

"That's the hard part of being Morris Koenig," she said, her voice reflective. "You'll want to use your resources and abilities to serve yourself, but if you do, you'll mess it all up. You have to be willing to let go of the things that have to happen."

I sighed impatiently. "Sometimes being Morris Koenig is a major buzzkill. 'Oh, here's a time machine and a load of supernatural abilities,'" I said in sarcastic voice. "'But don't you dare be selfish and use them.'"

Roxy laughed and punched my arm. "There it is – the Koenig tendency to be overly dramatic."

"It doesn't seem overly dramatic to me." I sniffed.

"Never does to your dad either."

"What about you?" I asked. "Where do you and Levi go from here?"

She didn't answer me. But her eyes left my face and found the little hill by the creek. I didn't have to look to know what was there.

"The graves. *Your* graves."

She watched me as I worked out the details.

"I always thought you died of old age in the past. Isn't that why the graves are ancient?"

She looked down at her folded hands.

"I can see the part of your mind you're trying to hide. That's not how you die, is it?"

"Morris, when your father and I die, there will be no regret, not even a shadow of doubt in our minds. We will embrace that day willingly. We have lived our whole lives for one thing."

"But you're not going to tell me what it is."

"Nope. It isn't something you need to know yet."

I gave up. There was no use trying to change her mind. My mother was the most stubborn creature that had ever lived.

"I love you, Mom."

She hugged me fiercely. "I love you more. Go bond with Jamie. The rest will work itself out at the right time."

Jamie and I had our bonding ceremony two days later.

The council wasn't happy. They didn't want to approve our match, but Grandmother reminded them it wasn't their place to prevent bonds. Leona had done that, after all, and look where it had gotten her people.

They agreed in the end. But they didn't agree to approve of Jamie. She had a hard road of proving herself ahead of her.

A year after we bonded, she launched the BioDroid program. As Jamie was herself, the Droids were controversial. Half of the council wanted them, half of them were opposed to the methods used to make them. If I was being completely honest, it was unsettling to watch her collect the dead from the SkyJack battles or the old who volunteered their bodies. Even more to watch her preserve and sculpt them into warriors armed with metal and tech.

But trouble only simmered, like a storm brewing in the distance that never seemed to come closer, for a long time.

As for me, as soon as Jamie was mine for good, I set to work. I made elaborate charts that I hung all over the dwelling we shared with Grandma. I studied time periods and made short time travel bursts to check on the timeline I was constructing. I labored over Unalterables until I learned to recognize them just by the sight of them, as a sort of aura that faintly glowed around the event in question. I became obsessed with my duty of saving the past. I memorized thousands of names from the 1600's to the 2100's, hoping to recognize the ancestors and put names with faces in my travels.

I'd like to say that Jamie and I had a perfect union. But it was easy for us both to get so involved in our projects we didn't spend time together. There were times where we grew apart and began to fight. Many times, I would have to return to her and apologize, and set my mind to make her the priority. She did the same for me.

After one reunion, she began to lose her appetite and feel sick. I was worried something was wrong with her. I ran a lot of diagnostics on her until Grandmother stopped me.

"Morris," she said with a gentle smile and a touch on my arm. "There's nothing wrong with her."

Sephora Koenig was born nine months after. Sophie. When Jamie reached for her and held the squirming new life in her arms, I thought my heart would explode from all the love I felt for both of them.

But my daughter's birth only made me more determined to solve the problems of the ancestors. If I didn't, she might never exist. Jamie might never come to me. I had to make sure that everything turned out the way it was supposed to go.

Then my life took a desperate plummet.

When our baby was not even a year old, a BioDroid malfunctioned. The out-of-control droid went on a mad rampage, wounded several, including children, and killing one of our respected men, an engineer in the Arena who was crucial to the set-up of the time manipulator.

The council didn't take it well. They blamed Jamie and some even accused her of doing it on purpose because she was still loyal to the SkyJacks. But Arabella talked them out of putting her on trial in the Arena. She gave us hope.

After that, my grandmother sent Jamie on a secret mission. I don't know why she didn't send me instead, but she didn't even tell me. She sent Jamie back to 1874, to the promenade deck of the reservoir, to a fallen Arabella who was bleeding from a head wound that needed immediate healing.

The way Jamie told it later, when she was called to testify, was this:

"I came through just as the portal window was closing. Levi was trying to heal her, desperately infusing her with healing energy. They were both lit up with blue light and energy. But she didn't respond, and he eventually had to leave her there and jump through the portal before it closed all the way.

"When the portal went dark, only Arabella was left on the promenade. All of Joe's army had disappeared and all of the Transient and Roxy's army had gone through to 2074 to defeat Leona. I went to her and used the revive injector. She woke up. I managed to finish the healing Levi had started."

"And did you know that use of the untested revive injector was forbidden?"

Jamie nodded.

Christiana Beckett shook her head. "Why? Why would you do something so reckless? Who gave it to you?"

"I did it to save Arabella Eisen. And I will not reveal where I got it."

I knew where she got it. From Arabella Eisen herself. But the council held the trial while Arabella was gone. She was somewhere in time and unable to speak up for Jamie. And Jamie refused to point the finger at her.

"Then you leave us with no choice."

The second council member, the one tasked with replacing me as Shepherd in the proceedings, came forward. "For the crime of going against the word of the council and using the time manipulator without the authorization of the council, as well as the crimes committed by your droids, you are sentenced to death in the time stream."

My world might as well have ended.

Jamie's features were determined and wary. Her eyes were wide and her fists clenched at her sides. She stood in front of the manipulator and waited.

"This is all wrong!" I yelled. "How can you punish her for saving lives? For saving all of us! Is this what we've become?" I stepped closer to the council members, who stood around the manipulator with solemn faces. "We cannot kill *her*, of all people! She is the one who will save us. She is the only one who understands the BioDroid tech. You *can't* do this."

"Move out of the way or join her in her sentencing," Christiana Beckett, the council physician, said.

A BioDroid pulled me back. I couldn't move, but I could call to her. I could continue my desperate protest. And I did.

"Jamie Salvatore of the Transient," Christiana said stiffly. "Speak thoughts to be remembered, if you have any."

Jamie was thoughtful for a long moment. "Not to save our leader, Arabella Eisen, would have been a mistake. If I had to choose again, I would still go back and revive her. If you're killing me for that crime, I'd rather it be me than her. I accept the exchange, but you should reevaluate our procedures for justice, for the good of our future. For the good of my daughter…" Her voice trailed off, swallowed by emotion. She took a deep breath and stood rigidly in front of the manipulator, her eyes closed. "Take care of our baby, Morris."

"I love you, Jamie." My voice broke as my throat tightened. I twisted and managed to break free of the droid. I ran to her.

The council members moved to stop me, but for some reason Christiana had mercy on me. She waved me on and turned her back on us. "Go ahead and say your goodbyes."

I was trying to think of a way to use the opportunity to save her, but Jamie interrupted my train of thought by bringing her hand to my cheek. For all the times that my calm had been used on her, now she calmed me.

"You'll be okay." She smiled. I felt breathless at her beauty.

"I can't let them do this," I whispered desperately.

"You're never alone," she promised. "I'll always be there."

I shook my head, my resolve weakening at her tender touch.

"You have a job to do. You have to keep going. You're the only one who can save them all."

"Stand back," Christiana called as a row of BioDroids stepped forward. At once they all projected lasers toward Jamie, the beams immediately possessing her body. She went limp, but the beams kept her upright and deposited her body in the light of the time manipulator. She disappeared with a violent shudder.

The BioDroids shuffled away, emotionless and guiltless, with the same burdened expression of death they always wore.

"Let our ways be preserved by the difficult task of justice." Christiana spoke with authority.

"Let it be so," the council members responded. But some of their voices lacked the usual conviction.

"Jamie!" I cried. My spirit was burning up with hers. I didn't want to carry on. I didn't want to understand. I wanted Jamie with me. I turned furious eyes on the members of the council, who suddenly seemed sheepish.

"I hate you all. You'll pay for this."

Twenty-Three

Circle 'round the gravestones
Look left and then look right
A prism in your pocket
Two rainbows both in sight.

I've noticed that throughout history, people have made up nursery rhymes about the morbid. I've always wondered about this. It seems wrong, somehow, to reduce the melancholy tale of humanity into flowery little ditties children can sing as they romp in the afternoon sunshine.

But maybe it's our greatest act of love. We give them warnings about their futures in a poem, hoping they will remember the moral and not have to repeat the lesson their parents or grandparents had to learn the hard way.

I only wanted the best for my bunker kids, and I made up lots of these rhymes in those years I raised all those kids on my own. I wanted their play and their education to have some sort of meaning. I knew they would have to build a new world. I hoped they would be ready to pursue it with maturity.

There's nothing worse than a society of adults who never grew up. When children are taught they are the center of the universe and their happiness comes before everyone else's, a terrifying culture is born. I knew my contribution to the new age would be small in comparison to the thousands of refugees and sky dwellers, but I wanted the Transient people, starting with my bunker kids, to know the importance of following. They wouldn't get their way every time a decision was made. They would learn to respect the one in charge and obey. In the bunker, I would listen to their complaints and take their suggestions into account, but in the end, only one could be in charge and make decisions. I was the one who had to do it since I was the adult.

But I hadn't always been the adult. I had learned to follow as well.

"Morris, are you going to stay with us for good?"

Thirteen-year-old Roxy hadn't spoken in a long time. I looked up at her. In the past few months, she had changed. I still expected to see the skinny girl with the fierce expression staring up at me with a child's eyes. But she had shot up at least six inches in the past year. She was becoming a woman.

I had to be honest with her. She needed to know what to expect. "My time here is almost up. Then you'll be in charge."

She frowned, but she didn't throw a fit like she would have before. She only narrowed her eyes and kept moving along the dark street, staying off the sensor pads built into the smart streets.

My mother was growing up fast. She had no idea that so much was about to happen.

"Sum it up for me," she said, her breathing labored as we jogged along in the dark. "What does it mean to be a leader?"

I considered her question. I wanted to tell her that leading was sacrifice. Like my father, Levi, had done for me when he met me in the alley and gave me all his strength to save me and died in the process.

I wanted to remind Roxy of what she would one day do in the citadel, taking my Sophie's death in the chair. That was leadership.

159

Or I could tell her about Jamie, giving her life only to receive it back again when the timeline was made right. The prism cast two rainbows. I could remember a life with her and a life without, both equally clear.

That was leadership, right?

But I couldn't tell her those things. My little bunker mother wasn't ready to know the details. So I said it a different way, and meant every word just as much.

"Love the Life-Giver and find out who he is. Love your people. Use your gift to take care of them."

"My gift?"

"You know what I mean."

She liked to pretend she didn't have her secret ability. I had let her get away with it when she was a child, but now it was time to harness her power. She would need it in the coming days.

"Roxy, there's something you can do that no one else can. Everyone has a spark of genius, but hardly anyone ever does what they could with it. Genius is found in passion. Take what you know that no one else knows and develop it. Don't be afraid of it."

"I'm not afraid."

I smiled. "You're terrified."

I took her hand, and she frowned at me. I knew I hadn't convinced her yet. I squeezed her fingers. "You'll be okay."

She sighed. "I guess I don't have a choice but to move forward."

"No, you don't. And neither do I."

She hesitated, but finally nodded. "I guess we better get on with it."

She ran ahead of me, and I stopped to watch her bound back to the sensor at the bunker entrance. I tried to swallow back the sudden lump in my throat. My voice only came out as a whisper.

"I love you, Mom."

Epilogue

My life was supposed to end when I went back to 2074. I was supposed to be stabbed in an alley. I had seen it in my travels, and I had marked it as the date of my death. I had known it was to protect my daughter, Sophie, and I was eager to get there and save her.

The only thing in all of my time travels that took me by surprise was the moment my father showed up at my death. My spirit had nearly sapped out. I was prepared to meet the Life-Giver until blue energy was all around me and in me, and my life was being restored.

I knew the life wasn't mine. The essence that revived me belonged to Levi. It was my father's life, given for me. Freely offered in exchange for his mortality.

Having your father die for you when his face is still youthful and his body is still strong marks you. It never leaves my mind.

Jamie was restored to Sophie and me. Just like the prism that casts two rainbows, we can remember two distinct lives – one where we had to go on without her, and another one where she was present for every moment. I brought her back because Levi brought me back. To see her with her grown daughter and her grandchildren is one of the gifts my father gave me the day he decided the future shouldn't die for the past.

I brought the bodies of my parents home. I carried them through time, one and then the other, and brought them to the quiet spot beside the creek. I dug the graves next to their ancient markers, made for them when they disappeared from their lives in seventeenth century New York.

When it came time to close the death pods and return their bodies to the earth, I put my hand on Roxy's hair, still long and soft and as stubbornly wavy as it ever had been.

"Sleep now, Mom." My whisper carried through the breeze and somehow seemed to fly upward, to where she was in worlds beyond. "I'll watch over you. Like I always did."

I like to think I've done that. I can see their graves from my bedroom window. I stand still and consider them every morning when I rise. I see the evidence that they lived when I look in the mirror. I see Roxy's flashing eyes in my granddaughter, and Levi's laughing brows in my grandson. They live on.

You're never alone. I will always be there.

Life gives life. Death is not the end. And family is the most important investment to see that good goes on.

This has been the story of a family. The story of a love that was so strong it bonded enemies together. It is the story of a family that fought for freedom, and still fights every day to keep that freedom alive. I hope when I am gone and my descendants wonder what I was like, that those who remember will say I did my duty. Not for recognition, but for love.

I hope they will remember our story and stick by the ones they love. I pray our people will go on.

This ends the data file of Morris Koenig, son of Levi and Roxy, father of Sephora and husband of Jamie.

The End.

ACKNOWLEDGMENTS

Thank you, readers. You have made this journey so much fun. I love your enthusiasm and the element you add to the Transient Series that just couldn't be there without you.

With all my heart, I dedicate this final chapter to you.

ABOUT THE AUTHOR

M.K. Parsons is an asker of questions, a thinker of thoughts, and a fangirl at heart. Her word-loving obsession developed early. She has always been a storyteller.

Beside her husband and children, she is also in love with questions disguised as books, goose bump-inspiring music, and of course, the crafting of worlds and far off people and places, where the only limit is the size of the imagination.

CONNECT WITH M.K. PARSONS ONLINE AT:

mkparsons.com
facebook.com/authormkparsons
https://www.goodreads.com/authormkparsons
twitter.com/MK_Parsons
pinterest.com/QuirkyAuthor/ (check out the Transient, Paradox, Relativity and Lineage boards!)

Keeping in mind this is an Indie project dependent on word of mouth, please leave your reviews for the Transient Series on Amazon and Goodreads today and spread the word!